HOW TO ARCHER

HOW TO ARCHER

THE ULTIMATE GUIDE TO ESPIONAGE AND STYLE AND WOMEN AND ALSO COCKTAILS EVER WRITTEN

By Sterling Archer

HarperCollins books may be purchased for educational, business, or sales promotional use. For information, please e-mail Special Markets Department at SPsales@harpercollins.com

FIRST EDITION

Designed by Jason Li and Casey Willis
Page Layout by Ashley Halsey

Library of Congress Cataloging-in-Publication Data

ISBN 978-0-06-206631-2

14 15 16 OV/RRD 20 19 18 17 16

for Shedley

CONTENTS

Section Six: How to Pay for It

FOREWORD

When HarperCollins first approached me to write the foreword to Sterling's little book, I must admit that I was more than a bit taken aback. Not quite aghast, but definitely shocked. For one thing, Sterling has never been much of a reader. In fact, to the best of my knowledge, the only things he ever read growing up were pornographic comic books (we used to call them "Tijuana bibles," but I'm sure that's no longer considered polite, what with all these immigrants driving around everywhere in their lowriders, listening to raps and shooting all the jobs). So the thought of Sterling writing an actual book? With words? Yes, I was definitely shocked.

I was also surprised to learn that HarperCollins wanted a "how-to" book for spies and didn't ask *me* to write it. Needless to say, I have far more experience in all areas of espionage than Sterling will ever have. I also think I could have brought a great deal of profound wisdom and unique insight to such a book, due to my being not only a single mother, but also—and more importantly—an incredibly successful woman in a field almost entirely dominated by men. It probably would have been an inspiration to little girls and young women all over the world.

Instead, I just assume you'll be getting crudely drawn maps to every whorehouse on the planet, accompanied by a step-by-step guide about how to rid oneself of pubic lice. Which is all just as well, as far as I'm concerned: I am currently penning my memoirs—*Secrets and Silk: The Malory Archer Story*—and don't wish to water down the brand.

Malory Archer
New York, New York

PREFACE

My life has basically been one amazing story after another. So when HarperCollins begged me to write a book for them, I naturally assumed they meant a memoir. Something along the lines of John Huston's *An Open Book*. Or some other book. And since the publishing business has been circling the drain for a while now, it made sense to me that HarperCollins would be eager to publish a book that would sell literally tons of copies. Also, to be frank, I've been living well above my means for pretty much my entire adult life, which made the thought of millions upon millions of dollars in book royalties more than a little appealing to me.

And so I agreed to take a lunch meeting, to which I brought a rough outline (hastily scribbled on a sheaf of cocktail napkins) of my thrilling life. The two editors from HarperCollins, turns out, were actually editrices.[1] This being the publishing world, neither was what you'd call "mildly attractive." One

1 It also turns out that an editrix—the plural of which is editrices—is just a woman editor.

was pretty mousy, the other sort of squat and boxy and mannish, almost like a young Gertrude Stein. But not nearly as—well yeah, about that ugly.

Fast-forward five martinis.[2]

Somewhere between martinis three and five, apparently, I said something that made Gertrude Junior storm out of the restaurant. Or I repeatedly made elephant noises every single time she tried to talk. It's all pretty hazy. Anyway, I thought the book deal was dead on arrival. Right up until the mousy one—utterly disarmed by a combination of white Zinfandel and Archer pheromones—put her hand on my knee and asked if we could continue the meeting at my place.

I'm (at least) seven martinis to the good at this point. I'm also thinking about John Huston, and about how—even though he was a ninety-year-old Mexican hermit when he wrote his memoirs—he probably got laid a bunch of extra times when they were published (which, by that point in his life, was just padding his stats). And so I pour the boozy little editrix into a cab and take her back to my place, thinking I'll cement the book deal by doing a little stat-padding of my own. But was I in for a surprise once I got her into the bedroom. Because you know how in the movies, when the mousy librarian type takes off her glasses and shakes down her hair, and it turns out that all this time she was ridiculously smoking hot?

This was not that. At *all.*

But by this point I really want HarperCollins to publish my memoirs. And since this pale, timid, and also somewhat (it's hard to even say this) nether-regionally-unkempt woman seemed to be the only means to that end, I bit the bullet and

---

[2] Plus the (at least) two that I'd had in the cab on the way over.

gave her the same mind-blowing Archer experience that I've spent a lifetime sharing with beautiful and exotic women the world over.[3]

Twice I thought she'd died. This was not the surprising part.

The surprise came later, after I had signed the contract and lay in bed (and she staggered around looking for her clothes and just generally not leaving), when I made an offhand joke:

"Don't worry, um . . . gorgeous. I won't put this in my memoirs."

And she hops around to face me—she was hopping around, trying to get her panty hose on, not realizing that why would any self-respecting woman wear *panty hose*?—and she goes:

"Memoirs? No, we want a *how-to* book. For spies."

"A how-to book?! A book can't teach someone *how to* be equal parts deadly and sexy! That's like asking a cobra to write a book about *how to* be a cobra!"

"Well, I'm sorry, but a how-to book is what you just signed a contract to write."

I pause, thinking about my options. And about money. And John Huston. And cobras.

"Could it have a chapter *about* cobras?"

"Um . . . sure. So listen, I've gotta run but . . . will you call me sometime?"

"Um . . . sure."

And so a how-to book it is. Whatever. But I can tell you right now it's nowhere near as exciting as my memoirs would have been. Especially since HarperCollins totally fucked me on the entire chapter about cobras. But if you like this book but also want to read a much *better* book, you should convince

---

[3] Including, simultaneously, two actual princesses. Sisters. Not proud of it. (Just kidding, I totally am.)

HarperCollins they should publish my memoirs. Maybe start some sort of petition, or a letter-writing campaign. Or, better yet, maybe give that mousy editrix a call.

Because God knows I didn't.

Sterling Archer

The Long Bar, Raffles Hotel, Singapore[4]

[4] I'm actually at the office. The Raffles banned me *years* ago.

INTRODUCTION

Just so we're clear, I didn't want to write a how-to book.[5]

Because I'm pretty confident that any book I write will be a runaway bestseller, get translated into about a thousand languages, and wind up on the shelves (though not for very long) of every bookstore from Hoboken to Hanoi. And so I ask you: what do you think's going to happen when I go *mano a mano* with some enemy agent who's read the trade secrets of Sterling Archer, the world's greatest secret agent?

Answer: I will shoot him in the face.

But the fact that he (or she—let's be honest, I've shot a woman before) has read this book and gotten a rare glimpse into the mind of Sterling Archer, the world's greatest secret agent, might give said aforementioned enemy agent crucial

5 Or an introduction to one, for that matter.

insight into my thinkings and doings at a critical moment (i.e., right about the time I would normally shoot him in the face).

This could make my job harder.

And while there are many things to like about being a devastatingly handsome, martini-drinking, jet-setting, model-banging, world's greatest secret agent, hard work isn't one of them. If I wanted to work hard, I'd be a farmer. Albeit a devastatingly handsome one. So even though my contract with (the man-hating, unkempt überfeminists at) HarperCollins makes it abundantly clear that I am legally bound—especially now that I've spent the advance—to write a how-to book, I am doing so only because said aforementioned contract is apparently iron-fucking-clad.

But whatever. I bloom where I'm planted.

SECTION ONE

HOW TO SPY

Just to reiterate, I think this whole thing is a bad idea. Especially this section. In addition to possibly enjeopardizing my life at some point in the future, sharing my secrets of tradecraft is wildly irresponsible: I bet this book won't be in stores twenty minutes before some dumb idiot kid catches himself on fire trying to make a Molotov cocktail (see *Molotov Cocktail,* page 84). But that's HarperCollins's problem. And apparently they have the best lawyers in the entire world.[6]

Thus, for the first time ever, I will now reveal many of the secret techniques which have helped make me, Sterling Archer, the world's greatest secret agent. In the world.

[6] So good luck with your lawsuit, anguished mother of that dumb idiot kid who caught himself on fire.

GENERAL TRADECRAFT

My contract—clearly and repeatedly—states that I am required to deliver a manuscript of no less than 30,000 words. And so the book you just bought[7] is going to have exactly 30,000 words in it.[8] The good news is that this word-processing software keeps a running tally of each and every word that I type. Like this one and this one and this one and this one and this one and this one.

The bad news is that there is absolutely no way I can teach you how to be even a *regular* secret agent—let alone an incredibly stylish one—in 30,000 words. And you can just forget about learning how to become the world's *greatest* secret agent. For one thing, that job's already filled. By me. For another thing, a lot of being the world's greatest secret agent is just instinct.

And I cannot teach you how to sense danger, like a dog can sense if there's a ghost in the house. I cannot teach you how to know, quite possibly before he knows it himself, what

[7] And which you better not just be reading in the store.

[8] And I just found out that footnote words count, so get ready for plenty of these. Blah blah blah blah blah.

your enemy's next move will be. I cannot teach you how to recognize the precise moment in the evening when the beautiful woman sitting across from you at the baccarat table will decide that—less than one hour from now—she is going to let you do things to her body that just this very morning would have been utterly abhorrent to her. If she could have even imagined them.[9]

What I can (and am contractually obligated to) do is paint it all for you in broad strokes. We won't be able to cover everything, and what we do cover we probably won't cover all that well, but at least you'll have some faint notion of what it is that I actually do for a living. Which is—as I may have already mentioned—be Sterling Archer, the world's greatest secret agent. In keeping with the broad-strokes concept, let me first prime the canvas, if you will, by defining a few core concepts about intelligence gathering for you, to wit and thusly:

At its most basic level, intelligence gathering is getting someone to show and/or tell you something that they should not, in fact, show and/or tell you. This is not unlike getting a woman to show and/or tell you that she has two kids with her soon-to-be ex-husband, the divorce from whom has not yet been finalized. You obviously don't care about her still being married (see recipe for *Mint Julep*, page 82), but the two kids are a definite, possibly asthmatic, deal breaker.[10]

And so intelligence gathering is divided into two general

---

9 Which, unless she happens to be a well-seasoned Saigon whore who lived through the Japanese occupation of French Indochina, she probably could not.

10 This is actually one of the things that I love about my job: the overlap of skill sets between my personal and professional lives. Knowing how to create an elaborate and well-crafted cover story to establish my *bona fides* when I'm undercover, for example, comes in incredibly handy when I need to blow off some clingy stewardess.

categories: human intelligence (or HUMINT) and signals intelligence (or SIGINT).

Signals intelligence gathering relies on a variety of electronic devices: radios, satellites, um, I suppose the telephone would fall under this heading . . . look, I'll be honest: I don't know much about SIGINT. That's for the lab-coated geeks in ISIS SIGINT Control. Those pathetic little men with slide rules sticking out of their pocket protectors, wearing ties with short-sleeved shirts. I'm not kidding: they actually wear ties with short sleeves. I guess the short sleeves are more practical attire for what they do all day, which I can only assume is masturbate under their desks while looking at hobbit-porn on the internets. The point is, I know about as much about SIGINT as those fist-glazing nerds know about what a clitoris looks like.[11] The whole concept—by which I mean signals intelligence, not that mysterious and magical, sometimes mauve, sometimes brown, amazing little pleasure bean known as the clitoris—is

---

11 I.e., very little, if anything.

incredibly boring to me. Which is why I focus my considerable talents in the area of human intelligence.

Human intelligence, as its name implies, is gathered from humans. Also known as people. Sometimes, but not always, these people are exotic, stunning *femmes fatales*, and I gather intelligence from them during or after sex.[12] Sometimes these people are men, who are usually either oily little Peter Lorre types (who can easily be bribed or intimidated into giving me information) or evil, Van Dyke–bearded masterminds with surprisingly big muscles (whom I usually have to fight, in a fairly elaborate set-piece, toward the end of whatever mission I'm on).

But sometimes the situation calls for something besides sex or fighting. When that happens, in addition to just sort of mentally disengaging from the entire mission, I am forced to use one or more of the numerous espionage techniques at my disposal:

BRIBERY

You probably already know what this is. I try not to rely on bribery too heavily, for two reasons: one, it's pretty boring. Two, ISIS has this whole big voucher process where you have to sign out the money, which they then count—like every *single* dollar—on Mother's desk, and the whole time she's just smirking at you with that smirky little smirk on her smirkly smirking face.

[12] I will leave the puerile "loose lips" joke to you. Mainly because I couldn't think of one. Wait . . . no, it's gone.

CUTOUT

A cutout is just a go-between, who goes between (I just got that) two intelligence agents. The cutout, if compromised, cannot in turn compromise the mission, because he doesn't know who is supplying the information, who is receiving the information, or even what the information is. Actually, reading back over that I'm not sure the concept was ever properly explained to me. Because that doesn't seem like it would work, does it? How does he know where he's going?

DEAD DROP

A dead drop is a secret location that makes it possible for two (or more) agents to exchange information without having to meet in person. One agent places the information[13] in the dead drop—for example, a mailbox. He then uses a prearranged signal to alert a second agent that a drop has been made— for example, a small red flag on the outside of the . . . Goddamn it. An hour of research. To basically just learn how the U. S. Postal Service works.

DISGUISES

I'm not a huge fan of using disguises. For one thing, if I'm being completely honest, I rely a lot on my looks. For a bunch of stuff. Mostly getting laid. So I'm never eager to put on shabby clothes and some old-guy makeup and a big fake nose. Or whatever. That being said, I *will* throw on the occasional false mustache.

---

13 And not just information. Any number of items may also be placed in a dead drop: sticks of chewing gum, some polished pennies, twine, a spelling-bee medal, an old pocket watch, carved wooden miniatures of children . . . It just depends on how much free time you have on your hands, and how far you're willing to go to lure those delicious children into your creepy old house. And I just assume the more free time you have, the more you want those yummy little cherubs.

And not just when I'm undercover: sometimes I'll just put one on and walk around the apartment, yelling at Woodhouse with an Armenian accent. Because, for reasons as yet unknown to me, this literally scares him to death.[14]

DOUBLE AGENT

A double agent is an operative who merely *pretends* to spy on one intelligence agency (Agency A) on behalf of a second intelligence agency (Agency B) but is in reality loyal to the first intelligence agency (Agency A). And I'm already confused, so here's a brief example:

Let's say I'm in Moscow, doing my thing. I get captured by an incredibly sexy KGB agent—let's call her Anya—who not only has perfect breasts but is also into all the same stuff I'm into. It's like she totally gets me. Anya then attempts to "turn" me—convince me to spy on ISIS for the KGB—using a combination of money, sex, a totally dude-like interest in lacrosse, and being at least somewhat open to the idea of anal. I agree

14 Or figuratively—whatever. Sorry, I forgot you were William Safire.

to spy on ISIS for the KGB. But in reality I just *pretend* to do so, and in fact spy *on*, and pass *dis*information *to*, the KGB *for* ISIS, during my bimonthly trips to Moscow. And bimonthly actually works out pretty well for me, because Anya's hot, but she's also a little crazy, and it turns out she was just stringing me along on the whole anal thing anyway. So it's not like I'm looking for anything super-long-term here.

A *redoubled agent* is a double agent (ostensibly spying for Agency B, in reality still loyal to Agency A) who has been discovered by the secondary controlling agency (Agency B) and then forced to actually spy on Agency A *for* Agency B, which he was supposed to be doing all along. That's also a bit complicated, so using the lovely Anya again, let's see how that might play out:

I'm back in Moscow, spying *on* the KGB *for* ISIS. Things with Anya are going just okay: we're both pretty busy with work, she's (rightfully) a bit suspicious about what I do with my evenings when I'm not with her, and to be honest, the sex just isn't what it used to be. We get in some huge stupid fight about I can't even remember what, she starts throwing my stuff all over the bedroom, and the next thing I know, we're both staring at these secret ISIS codebooks that were in my Hermès grip (which is now so scuffed as to be totally unusable). I am exposed. So, not wanting to end this lovely evening with a 7.62mm Tokarev slug in my brain, I agree to become a *redoubled agent* and spy *on* ISIS *for* the

KGB. Anya, for her part, agrees that she has trust issues and promises to see someone about it. The anal question, *for now,* is left unresolved.

A *triple agent*—not to be confused with a redoubled agent[15]—is simply an intelligence operative who works for three separate intelligence agencies. A *triple-double* has something to do with basketball, or maybe hockey. I wouldn't know: I'm more of a lacrosse man, myself.

FALSE FLAG

This technique derives its name from pirate times, when the pirates would drive around in their pirate ships, drinking gimlets and flying a non-terrifying, non-skull-and-crossbones festooned flag. The Italian flag, for example. Then some non-pirate ship—probably stuffed to the boat-rafters with slaves and rum—would see the pirates and, thinking they were just some cool Italian guys who probably know where the party is, wave for them to come over there.

But just when the pirates got within grappling-hook range . . . *bam!* Out comes the ol' Jolly Roger, and then the pirates would spend the rest of the afternoon raping the woolen pants off everybody.

Today a false flag operation is when an operative from one intelligence agency (Agency A) executes a mission against a second agency (Agency B) while posing as an operative for a *third* agency (Agency C) causing Agency B to cast blame on Agency C. Nobody gets raped.[16]

---

15 A redoubled agent could, in theory, be redoubled an infinite number of times. In practice, however, somebody from either Agency A or Agency B usually gets tired of his bullshit after about three times and puts one in his ear.

16 Unless Agency A is a pirate ship.

HONEYPOT

By far my favorite intelligence-gathering technique, the honeypot relies on a combination of seduction and blackmail. The Soviets are generally recognized as being the most skilled in the use of the honeypot, employing it with great success against Western agents all over the globe. The KGB term for a female agent used in a honeypot is a "swallow," which works on so many levels I don't even know where to begin.[17]

The first step in the honeypot is *seducing* an enemy agent sexually. Normally the "honey" in the "honeypot" is a woman, but this is not always the case: agents of the British clandestine services have traditionally been incredibly likely to be seduced by thin, handsome, nearly body-hairless young men with lips like soft plums. Oh, and cocks.

The second step in the honeypot is to *blackmail* the enemy agent by threatening to reveal the fact that he allowed himself to be seduced sexually.

If the honey is a woman, the threat of exposure must be predicated upon the fact that said enemy agent is specifically prohibited by his government or agency from sexually fraternizing with any woman belonging to a particular group or organization (female East German civilians, for example, or female KGB agents). Otherwise, the only thing he'd have to worry about—when the glossy black-and-whites of him getting a rim job from some gorgeous blonde showed up at his agency—is tearing his rotator cuff high-fiving everybody.

If the honey is a broody, flaxen-haired twink—with soulful eyes, the slightest hint of downy blond fuzz on his lower back, and an ass that would've made Lord Byron chew his own lips off—that's usually enough right there. You don't even need to

---

[17] It actually only works on one level. Which is as a joke about swallowing semen.

go to the trouble of making glossy black-and-whites: the (invariably British) agent will just assume that Stefan's camera phone fell out of his pocket while he was doing poppers in a toilet stall in some club.

The third step is *coercing* the enemy agent to do your bidding. Continue to do so until he is exposed as a double agent by his government and summarily executed.[18]

LICENSE TO KILL

This concept gets bandied about a great deal. But if you happen to mention it, some guy—not the highly trained intelligence agent standing next to you on the firing range as you both repeatedly ten-ring a Carlos the Jackal silhouette, just some random guy in a bar whose girlfriend is about three minutes away from going home with you—will blurt out how it's not actually a real thing. Well, guess what, genius: not only is it a real thing, but I just realized that I forgot to renew mine. And

18 Because I don't know why you were expecting this scenario to have a happy ending.

it's not like I don't have thirty dollars, but that's just totally out of line for a late fee.[19]

MOLE

Named after Morocco Mole—the loyal sidekick of intelligence-operative-slash-rodent Secret Squirrel—the mole, also known as an "agent in place," is one of the most important aspects of counterintelligence. The mole is an intelligence operative who works—for an extended period, sometimes decades—in the clandestine service of an *enemy* government (e.g., the United States) but who remains loyal to his *own* government (e.g., the Soviet Union). I used the United States as the dupe in that example because to the best of my knowledge, we've never been able to slip an American mole past those sneaky Reds. Conversely, it is estimated[*by whom?*] that three out of five American intelligence agents are, in fact, Russian spies.

That's obviously hyperbole (if that word means what I think it does), but as far as moles are concerned, the USSR has been kicking America's ass through its hat ever since WWII. In fact, the United States has only been able to successfully mount one mole operation in the past fifty years, which was Donnie Brasco. And which doesn't really count, because it was against Italy.

---

[19] Oh, and also, we're out of here, so tell your girlfriend to get her coat: I would, but I don't speak bridge-and-tunnel.

MOSCOW RULES

I don't know what this is.

UNARMED COMBAT

As Sterling Archer, the world's greatest secret agent, I am all too frequently required to defend my physical person-body from all kinds of various attackers and/or assailants. From the KGB to cuckolded husbands, I've been in physical altercations with just about everything on two legs.[20] Luckily for me, I have a veritable slew of arrows in my self-defense quiver. Not including actual arrows, which technically belong in the section on ranged weapons.[21]

But back to the quiver-slew: I have trained—or was supposed to have trained, but then it turned out the classes were just crazy-early in the morning—in numerous deadly martial arts. These trainings are as follows, in no particular order. Well, other than alphabetical. Turns out.[22]

---

20 And also, on one regrettable occasion, on one leg. But I don't take that kind of talk from anybody, disabled veteran or not. But thank you for your service.

21 If there even is one of those. After the whole cobra debacle, there's no telling what'll end up in this stupid book. Liars.

22 Thanks to my mousy little editrix. As she begins to rear her jealous, passive-aggressive, dandruffy little head.

AIKIDO

Japanese, I think. Maybe something to do with bamboo swords? No idea. This was one of those crazy-early-in-the-morning ones. Sensei guy was a dick. Did not train in this discipline.

BOXING

While I never trained as a boxer (mainly because it's not very practical for life-or-death situations), boxing is nonetheless an important part of my life: I like to get out to Vegas at least once a year for a heavyweight title bout. Because that's basically like the Oscars for hookers.

CAPOEIRA

Brazilian martial art combining hand-to-hand combat with music and dance. Seriously. It's essentially "samba krumping." I don't get it, didn't train in it, but it makes me wonder: who could make a street fight sexier than the Brazilians? Answer: some other, even sexier Brazilians.

GATKA

A Sikh martial art which uses swords, lances, javelins, bows and arrows, and something called a *bagh nakh*, which is what I imagine would happen if Freddy Krueger and some brass knuckles had a baby. Did not train in this discipline. Because I'll just say it: I was kinda scared.

HAPKIDO

I could not (well, chose not to) attend hapkido training, but I think Steven Seagal holds a ham-flavored belt in it. So if you ever need to fight Marlon Brando's fatter, more ponytailed doppelgänger, just call Steven Seagal and ask him how he would go about it. I just assume he would eat his opponent, while growling: "Om nom nom, I was in the CIA, nom nom nom . . ."

JUDO

Judo can be (and apparently usually is) translated as "the gentle way" or "the way of gentleness." Developed in Japan by a Japanese guy named Dr. Kanō Jigorō in the mid- to late-eleventh century BC,[23] judo relies on the principle of using an opponent's strength and/or momentum against himself. Awesome concept, right?

Yes. If some barefoot dude comes lurching at you in slow-motion wearing loose-fitting pajamas. Which, even though it's probably happened to me a dozen times (cuckolded husbands, above), doesn't mean they should build an entire martial art around it. Most of the time you can stop those guys dead in their tracks by just reminding them whose fault the whole situation really is: Did I make you spend so much time at the office? Did I make you play three rounds of golf last weekend? Answer: No, I didn't. I was too busy pinning your wife's ankles to her ears.

KARATE

I have not actually trained in karate, which I've often been quoted as calling "the Dane Cook of martial arts." However, I believe that Dane Cook has since become the Dane Cook of comparisons, so that now the joke has lost all meaning.[24]

KRAV MAGA

Krav Maga is Hebrew[25] for "Beat the shit out of it. Literally, until it shits." It's also where I hang my self-defense hat. Which

---

23 Give or take.

24 Also, the original joke was "the Applebee's of martial arts." Which, for numerous reasons, is a much better joke: there is nothing wrong with Applebee's per se; it's just readily available to the general public. Not unlike karate. Dane Cook, on the other hand—actually, you know what? Dane Cook is great. Love to work with him someday.

25 Or maybe Yiddish? One of those.

in this case is a yarmulke, because Krav Maga was developed in 1930s Czechoslovakia by a Jewish guy named Imi Lichtenfeld, who taught it to other Jews so that they could defend themselves against attacks by their anti-Semitic neighbors. When Israel achieved statehood in 1948, Lichtenfeld taught Krav Maga to the Israeli Defense Forces so that *Israel* could defend itself against attacks by its anti-Semitic neighbors.[26]

And I won't digress into geopolitics or religion or ideology (mainly because I don't care what you think about any of those things—or anything else, for that matter). But when it comes to fighting, who better to learn from than a people who have been beset, on all sides and for millions of years, by enemies who want nothing more than their complete and utter annihilation?

Answer: the Jews.[27]

KUNG FU

The way I heard it, Bruce Lee took this idea to ▇▇▇▇▇ so *he* could star in it. But they totally screwed him. And you know, not to take anything away from David Carradine, but still.

MUAY THAI

Thailand's national sport, Muay Thai, is a truly devastating form of kickboxing which utilizes not only the fists and feet, but also the knees and elbows. It is also another discipline *in* which I have not been trained, but *on* which I do like to gamble. Not unlike jai alai. *¡Vaya!*

---

26 I.e., every single other country in the whole entire Middle East.

27 Also a pretty good place to learn about history, music, that Sandy Koufax and Sammy Davis, Jr. were awesome, science, literature, and how to invent the atomic bomb. Plus, I think I already covered beating the shit out of people.

SAVATE

I never trained in this discipline, but *savate* is French for "face kick." And while the French have a reputation for being effeminate, beret-wearing cheese-nibblers, I think this is unfair. Because they also have a reputation for having the French Foreign Legion. So the next time you're feeling adventurous, walk into a bar in Algiers and call a Legionnaire a *putain de merde*. Then walk outside and feel around in the sand with your hands, trying to find your head.

ARCHER BY THE NUMBERS: UNARMED COMBAT

- Pounds per square inch needed to break a human collarbone (adult): 7
- Pounds per square inch needed to break a human collarbone (child): 11

(That's as far as I got because I read that statistic and got freaked out that someone actually researched that. And then I started thinking about why it takes more pounds of pressure to break a kid's collarbone, and all I can figure is it's because they're shorter. The collarbones, not the kids. Although I assume the test kids were also pretty short.)

WEAPONRY

As we learned in the section on unarmed combat, my entire body is essentially a weapon. I have killed men with my bare hands. I have killed a man with my bare feet. I have killed a man, albeit accidentally, with my bare knee. But as any secret agent worth his single-malt will tell you, the best way to keep a knife sharp is *to not use it*. Which was supposed to be a clever segue into the section on bladed weapons (below), but I guess now I have to explain what I meant by that, which is this: whenever possible, *avoid unarmed combat*. Because there's no sense breaking your hand on an enemy's head when you can just put a bullet in it. In fact, while you're at it, go ahead and double-tap that poor bastard: it's not like there's a bullet shortage.[28]

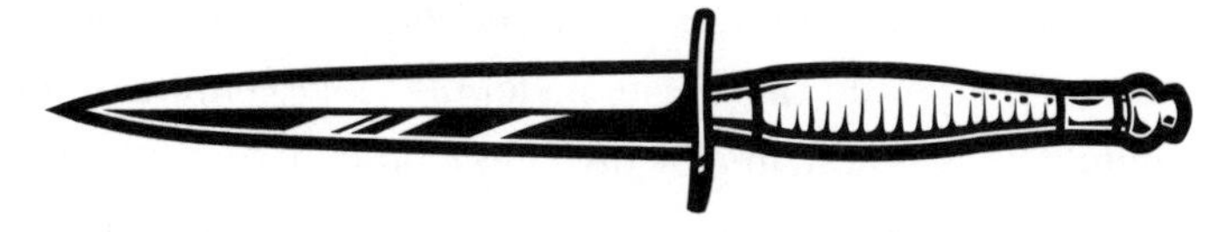

BLADED WEAPONS

I normally don't carry a knife, for two reasons. One: this may sound fussy, but I don't care for the way they affect the fall of my suit jacket. Two: God invented silencers for a reason.

If I feel that I need to carry a knife on a mission—which, again, is exceedingly rarely—it will, and can only, be a Fairbairn-Sykes Fighting Knife.

---

28 There was one a few years back, but apparently they've got that all straightened out now.

And say what you will about the British secret services (they're pussies, etc.), they know how to make a knife. I like the Fairbairn-Sykes for its proven ability to penetrate an enemy's rib-cage with minimal effort. And also for its heavy steel pommel, which is excellent for cracking open walnuts. If I'm ever in a forest or something.

Swords, especially samurai and/or ninja ones, are exceptionally cool. However, their use is of limited practical value to the secret agent, especially given the fact that somebody invented gunpowder about a million years ago. I have not trained in fencing (or vaginal hygiene), so if I am forced to use a sword in combat, I just swing it around like a baseball bat while screaming, at the top of my lungs: "There can be only one!" Which, if done correctly, is surprisingly effective.

After seeing the (shamefully Academy-snubbed) film *Road House*, I was intrigued by the idea of having a razor-sharp blade built into one of my handcrafted Italian shoes. I asked my Italian cordwainer[29]—Antonio Carbone of Casa di Scarpe Carbone—if it would be possible to have this done the next time he was resoling a pair of balmorals for me. Well, you would've thought I asked him if he could slap some bigger tits on *la Vergine Maria* and, while he was at it, maybe give her a little more *cuscino* for the *spingendo*. I've never seen a man so indignant in my life (a woman yes, but never a man). And although I've apologized repeatedly and profusely and Antonio says he's forgiven me, I can tell he thinks a little bit less of me. As a human being.

HANDGUNS

Go German or go home.

And yes, I know: they're a horrible people. But they also make excellent firearms. And while I'm sure many of you are of the opinion that one should always buy American, you're

---

29 Which you probably call a shoemaker. Because I want to murder you.

stupid. Because even though the Colt .45 ACP M1911A is an excellent sidearm - the design of which has remained almost totally unchanged since before WWI - it utterly ruins the lines of my suits. And I personally am not willing to sacrifice style for a teeny little bit of extra stopping power.

Which is why my service weapon is the Walther PPK. Chambered for the .32 ACP cartridge, my Walther has a magazine capacity of seven rounds, plus one in the chamber. And if whatever you're shooting doesn't die after you pump eight thirty-two-caliber slugs into it, it's probably a dragon.

While I am *extremely* fond of my Walther PPK (and if the good folks at Carl Walther GmbH Sportwaffen are reading this book and wish to contact me about becoming a corporate sponsor, I would be open to that), I usually carry a backup weapon. Which is also a Walther.[30] This weapon is an ultracompact, semiautomatic Walther TPH—chambered in .22 LR[31] and with a magazine capacity of six rounds, plus one in the chamber—which I keep in my underwear.

ASSAULT WEAPONS

Again, there's a reason why the Third Reich, at its peak, stretched from Leningrad to London: the Germans make good

30 Seriously, guys: Just gimme a call. I'm around.

31 The positive attributes of the .22 caliber cartridge, of which there are several, will be covered later.

guns. And yes, I know the Nazis lost WWII. I get the paper. But they lost because all the Wehrmacht officers were constantly being rotated off the front lines so they could return to Germany to have their uniforms altered—in a futile attempt to keep up with the constantly changing fashion trends of an unwinnable, two-front war—by Hugo Boss.[32]

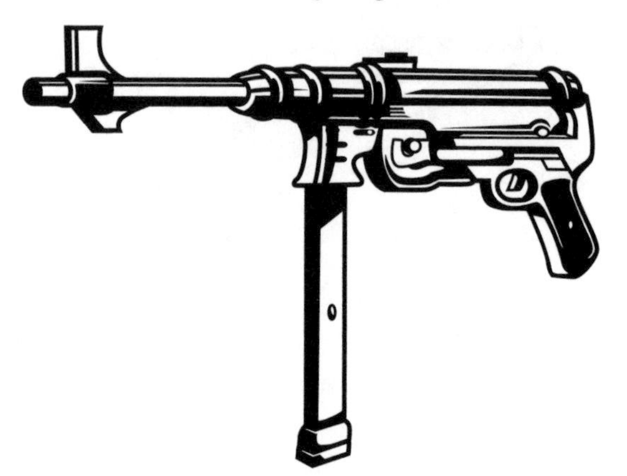

They did *not* lose because their assault weapons weren't awesome. So for my money (which is not actually my own personal money), when I need an assault weapon, I reach for either the MP 40 or the StG 44. And yes, it's a little creepy at first. But you get over it. Mainly because firing 550 rounds a minute out of either of these weapons gives you a gigantic boner.

My personal preference for German assault weapons notwithstanding, I would be remiss if I failed to mention that regime-toppling workhorse, the AK-47 (or its Chinese variant, the Type 56). Designed by Mikhail Kalashnikov in 1947, the AK-47 has a well-deserved reputation for being an exceptionally reliable weapon. It will perform under even the harshest conditions: you can get an AK-47 wet, you can get an AK-47

32 Some of which is true.

dirty—hell, you can drag it through a cranberry bog—and you will still be able to fire it accurately. But, while doing so, you will look like a rapper.

I should also take a moment to mention the Uzi. Which, in addition to being an accurate and reliable subcompact assault weapon with both a high muzzle velocity and an extremely high rate of fire, is yet another reason not to mess with the Jews.

FLARE GUN

While the flare gun—also known as a Very pistol—was originally designed for use as a signaling device, you can also use it to shoot people. People who then catch on fire.

EXPLOSIVES

No. I consider them sloppy.

OTHER WEAPONS

I could basically just start typing a list of nouns. Because if you have been trained properly, *anything* can be used as a weapon. Take my finely crafted Walther PPK, for example: at some point it will run out of bullets.[33] But when it does, guess what: it weighs twenty-three ounces.[34] Now guess what else weighs about twenty-three ounces. I'll tell you: a framing

---

33 Which I don't consider a design flaw. At all. If anything, this makes the Walther PPK even more spectacular.

34 Which is *perfect*.

hammer. Now guess what you wouldn't want to get smashed in the teeth with. I'll tell you: either of those.

And so, just look around. Chances are that within five feet of you, there are at least three items—not including your bare, muscular hands—that you could use to kill a person: your keys, a brassiere, an empty jeroboam of champagne, a billiard ball, an ivory-handled shoehorn, a stiletto heel, another empty jeroboam of champagne, a double-ended glass dildo, an entire set of barbecue tools . . . See? And that's just me looking at the stuff lying on or around my bed.

The point is, almost anything can be used as a weapon. And, as with many things in life, the only limit is your imagination: I once killed a guy with a gorgeous Raymor ashtray.[35]

ARCHER FUN FACT: WEAPONS

In the fourteenth century, the Ming Dynasty had a weapon called a Nest of Bees. It was a large tube filled with about three dozen rocket-propelled arrows. I bet you thought I was going to say "rocket-propelled bees," but no, it was just arrows. (*Just* arrows! LOL!!!)

35 Which I regret. Because the ashtray was a gift. From that same guy.

GADGETS

I don't care for this term. I feel it debases the professionalism of intelligence operatives, who are the bravest, most selfless public servants in the world and who put their very lives at risk every single day to keep freedom-loving peoples safe from tyranny and oppression. Also, it's very nearly impossible to use the term gadget without preceding it with the word nifty.

But I can't think of a better term. For a while I tried getting people to say spechnology (a clever portmanteau of "spy" and "technology"), but I couldn't get anybody to get on board for the big win. Anyway, as an ISIS agent I have access to a dizzying array of spechnological aids. Our in-house scientist, Dr. Algernop[36] Krieger, is constantly either inventing or improving devices with which to stun, kill, bedazzle, set on fire, confuse, or otherwise incapacitate enemy agents:

PEN GUN

Outwardly, the pen gun appears to be an innocent—though finely crafted—writing instrument (you can actually write with it if the nature of the device is ever called into question). Inwardly, however, the pen gun contains a single .22 caliber, subsonic, hollow-point cartridge (I call it the Mont Blam) which is

36 No, that's not a typo.

fired by depressing the pocket clip twice in rapid succession.[37]

I carry one, but I don't really consider it practical: If I want to shoot somebody, I use my service weapon. And if I have to enter a location where I will be searched for weapons, odds are they're not going to let me keep this bulky bastard, because *everybody* knows about pen guns.

I have used it to blow a broken cork out of a bottle of '38 Bâtard-Montrachet, however. Actually, that's inaccurate: the cork was blown *into* the bottle of Bâtard-Montrachet, along with a bunch of glass and a tiny bit of my fingertip. But, even though it was a chardonnay, I drank it.

SPY WATCH

I cannot *believe* a high-end timepiece company hasn't approached me about becoming a corporate sponsor yet. Every men's magazine I open, there's about fifty full-page watch ads, each starring some trout-shouldered golfer with his chin on his fist and a big gleaming watch on his wrist, gazing intently past the camera. Probably at some dude he wants to blow.

Seriously, a *golfer*? What marketing genius came up with *that* brilliant idea? Why not just strap your twenty-one jewel, Swiss-movement, sapphire-crystal, stainless-clad, waterproof-to-half-a-goddamn-mile chronometer on the limp and bony wrist of an *actor*, for Christ's sake?

---

[37] The subsonic .22 might seem like a rather vaginal caliber. But it's actually pretty great because, due to its low muzzle velocity, it doesn't produce a through-and-through wound: That little .22 slug enters the human body and then—like a kitten with its head stuck in a sock—just sorta slams around all over the place, smashing into everything and totally unable to escape. Only instead of a kitten, it's a bullet. And instead of all the expensive china and Waterford crystal on the table after a lavish dinner party, it's the liver and spleen and lungs. Either way, your hosts won't think it's funny.

Anyway, whatever. If I did have a spy watch, it would have a garrote concealed in the unidirectional bezel. But just talking about it makes me furious.

GARROTE

A garrote is a length of Damascus steel painstakingly hammered and folded and drawn about a million times by a Syrian blacksmith until it becomes a thin, yet incredibly high-tensile piece of wire that I could – if the ██████ Watch Co. didn't suck complete ass – conceal in the unidirectional bezel of my custom spy watch. Which I would then use to strangle the life out of ████████, the douchebag VP of marketing for the ██████ Watch Co., who won't return my calls.

CYANIDE CAPSULE

ISIS agents are required, at all times, to be equipped with two cyanide capsules—a primary capsule and a reserve, in the event the primary fails to activate properly—which are to be used if the agent faces imminent capture by the enemy. The capsules are actually ceramic crowns custom-molded to the agent's rearmost molars and designed to shatter when he/she bites down with a minimum of 150 pounds of force, causing nearly instantaneous death. Yeah, no thanks.

I had Krieger replace the cyanide in one of my capsules with Binaca, and in the other with Xanax. That way I'm ready for pretty much whatever the day may have in store for me.

HOLLOW COIN

These are neat. Fabricated in such a way as to be totally indistinguishable from an actual coin—down to its exact weight, *in micrograms*—the hollow coin can be utilized to stealthily carry or pass top-secret information, which is usually formatted onto microfilm or microchips.

I use mine as a conversation starter. With women I meet in bars. It's an excellent way to segue, more or less organically, into the fact that I, Sterling Archer, am the world's greatest secret agent. I then take these women home—or into the alley out back, or wherever—and screw them.

KNOCKOUT DROPS

I use these when the hollow coin doesn't work.[38]

KNOCKOUT GAS

Ditto. No, not really. Mainly because I'm not sure we even possess the technology to produce knockout gas. Yet. Which is why I constantly check the bulletin board at ISIS. To date, though, all I've gotten from my constant bulletin board-checkery is a used pair of inline skates.

ADRENALINE SYRETTE

Often I am required to secure covert ingress into a fortified enemy compound or embassy, or sometimes even a palace. These locations are normally patrolled by two or more giant and ferocious Rottweilers, which I must incapacitate using "hush puppies" (a combination of knockout drops and bacon). The adrenaline syrette is used to reawaken the dogs when I have completed my mission, to avoid alerting my enemies that their perimeter has been breached. The animals are temporarily disoriented when they awake, giving me ample time to

---

[38] I'm kidding! Jesus, lighten up, Joan Baez. First of all, I only use knockout drops when I need to incapacitate a sentry—human, Rottweiler, or some combination thereof—so that I may secure ingress into a fortified enemy compound with the goal of extracting either information or a prisoner, which/who will then provide me with the intelligence I need to keep *you* safe at home in your cheap, metal-framed bed, in which you're probably lying, right now, waiting for *Green Acres* to come on so you can masturbate to Ralph. Secondly, the hollow coin *always* works.

escape. I also like to use these on myself on the rare mornings that Woodhouse's Bloody Mary doesn't suffice.

NIGHT VISION GOGGLES

Love love love love love the night vision goggles. They are fantastic in the field, obviously, but what I really like to do is put them on and sneak into Woodhouse's room while he's asleep. Then I just sit by his bed and wait (but never for very long because, since he's a thousand years old, he gets up about fifty times a night to pee). Then he wakes up to see these glowing green orbs staring at him, which literally scares the piss out of him.[39] When he asks me what I'm doing, I say: "Nothing. Everything is fine. Go back to sleep, Woodhouse. Everything is fine."

X-RAY SPECS

Not a real thing. Grow up.

SMARTPHONES

I'm on the fence about smartphones. Call me a romantic, but there's just something about a tiny Minox camera or a tape recorder concealed in a fountain pen that just sends me. On the other hand, having this spechnology—plus maps, a video recorder, GPS, a currency converter, translation software, games, an accelerometer, *and* a telephone—combined into one slim device has done wonders for the fall of my suit jackets.

---

39 Yes, William, literally.

I mean, I've even got a Geiger counter app. It's just the lite version, though, so it only gives a reading of plus/minus 100 rems (or one sievert).

THE TACTLENECK®

While technically a garment, the Tactleneck®—an even cleverer portmanteau of "tactical" and "turtleneck"—is an indispensable piece of equipment, and one without which I would never consider embarking on a mission. Woven from only the purest Azerbaijani cashmere wool (dyed either black or slightly darker black), the Tactleneck® is flexible enough for me to throw deep, devastating punches, yet formfitting enough to not become caught in abseiling/rappelling gear. And after the mission, I just throw a smart blazer over it and I'm ready for a night on the town.

TACTICAL SUPPOSITORY

Inserted into the rectum before a mission if an intelligence agent believes he is likely to be subject to capture and/or search, the tactical suppository is a watertight, hollow titanium tube about four inches in length and one inch in diameter (or roughly the size of a pro linebacker's thumb). The suppository can be filled with microfilm, a set of tiny lockpicks and saw blades, local currency, poison, or any number of other items the agent may require on the mission. I was told that because a battery would take up too much interior space, the suppository cannot be made to vibrate.

And before you say: "Man, I'd *never* put anything up my butt! That's gay!" go read the book *Papillon*. Then go watch the movie they made out of it, which stars actual real-life United States Marine and race-car driver Steve McQueen.

Then go watch, in this order, *The Getaway*, *Le Mans*, *Bullitt*, *Junior Bonner*, *The Magnificent Seven*, and *The Great Escape*.

Then call Ali MacGraw and ask her who's gayer: Steve fucking McQueen, or you.

STELLAR NAVIGATION

Fuck off.

TACTICAL DRIVING

I do not drive an Aston Martin DB5.[40] Mainly because I don't have a vagina.[41]

When I do drive, I prefer at least 350 cubic inches of Detroit muscle under the hood. Something along the lines of, say, a Dodge Challenger. Or some other prospective corporate sponsor. Because I need to know that the power is there if I need it, coiled and ready to strike.

Not unlike a *cobra*.[42]

But the way I see it, if people were supposed to drive automobiles, John Henry Ford wouldn't have invented cabs. Or bourbon. Which was probably invented by some other guy. I don't know, I honestly don't really care, and as my editrix has

---

40 Like some other spies whom I could mention but will not.

41 Ditto.

42 The Shelby AC Cobra, while not an actual cobra, is nonetheless completely and utterly badass.

made abundantly clear, this is a how-to book, not a history book. So here's *how to* drive like a secret agent:

Big. Fast. Hard.

And no, the sexual innuendoes are not lost on me. This is me you're talking to. Or vice versa.[43] But many of the same principles that apply to sex also apply to tactical driving. I don't necessarily know what those principles are, but I do know that (unless you're Dan Tanna) you're not going to ask the car to move in with you. No matter how much junk is in the trunk.[44]

Oh, and also always try to back into a parking space. I think I remember hearing that.

BRIEF QUESTIONNAIRE #1

1. Who do you think would win in a fight between me and James Bond?
2. What?
3. Well, have you ever even *seen* me fight?
4. Because keep it up, tough guy . . . you just keep it up.

---

43 Is this an audio book? What are we doing?

44 Unnecessary weight in the car's trunk is actually undesirable: not only will random items stored in the trunk decrease your top speed and gas mileage, these items could become dangerous projectiles in the event of a collision.

OTHER VEHICLES

Sometimes, in my profession as the world's greatest secret agent, I am required to drive, captain, pilot, or otherwise conduce forwardly, vehicles which are not automobiles. These vehicles include, but are not limited to, the following, including:

AIRBOATS

I personally find airboats rather difficult to drive. That's because I'm constantly fidgeting around, trying to find a

comfortable position for my gigantic, throbbing, purple-veined erection. Oh my God, is there anything in the world more infinitely cool than a screaming airboat?! No! Because an airboat is what happens when some mad, brilliant Civil War scientist decides it might be pretty cool to mount a 700-horsepower aircraft engine on a lightweight aluminum johnboat. Which, when you think about it: how did the Confederates not win the war?

Plus, the seats on an airboat are generally mounted very high on its frame. And while this raises the vessel's center of gravity a bit higher than the ideal, it also makes it a lot easier to tear through the bayous, blasting the beady eyeballs out of every alligator in sight with an AR-15.[45]

SNOWMOBILES

Kinda rednecky. And those two-stroke engines aren't doing the ozone layer (or whatever Earth's giant, invisible space-blanket is called) any big favor. However, like most other things rednecks love (moonshine, tractor pulls, anal sex, boar hunting), snowmobiles are pretty dang fun.

FIAT 500

Technically an automobile. But the "500" refers to its engine displacement. In cubic *centimeters*. Which isn't all that impressive for a motorcycle, much less a two-door sedan. Seriously, whenever I see one of these at a stoplight in Italy, I always expect a bunch of midget *pagliacci* to clamber out and run all around the intersection, whacking each other with *sfilatini*.

---

45 That sentence makes it seem like the *alligators* have AR-15s. A chilling thought . . .

MOTORCYCLES

Although I am fantastic at riding them, and could probably do a wheelie for about a mile if I wanted to, my only real interest in motorcycles concerns the sidecar. Which is a cocktail.

AN ELEPHANT

I realize that an elephant is an animal. But I think it's perfectly reasonable to include elephants in a section about vehicles because I also realize that I've seen about a thousand skinny little brown dudes *riding around on* about a thousand elephants.

And no, genius, obviously not all at once.

Because that would mean I'm a handsome Roman centurion, gaping at Hannibal and the endless horde of elephant-riding Moors he's waltzing through the gap in the Pyrenees that I was supposed to be in charge of defending. And also wishing that I wore a tunic, like all the other centurions, because I just shit my pants.

Also: Indian elephants (the ones you can ride) have ears shaped like India. African elephants (the ones you most certainly *cannot* ride) have ears shaped like Africa.[46]

46 And yet you're going to sit there with a straight face and tell me you don't believe in intelligent design.

POISON

Poison sucks.

I'm not talking about the hair-metal band (which totally sucks) or the Bell Biv DeVoe song (which totally doesn't). I'm talking about the assorted pills, powders, capsules, liquids, sprays, and umbrella tips that spies use to kill other spies.

I've seen agents killed with everything from roach powder to radioactive pellets. Often these poisons are fast acting: if you got hit in the neck with a dart tipped with poison[47] from the tiny *Phyllobates terribilis*, also known as the Poison Dart Frog (holy shit—true story—I just this second got why they call them that) you'd be dead before you reached the end of this sentence.[48]

Other poisons are slow-acting: Let's say you're on a mission in some Eastern Bloc capital (doesn't matter which one—they're all crappy) and some potato- or cabbage-faced guy on the metro "accidentally" jabs you in the leg with his umbrella. You beat the shit out of him.[49] You complete your mission and fly back to the States. You go out with the stewardess you banged on the return flight. Turns out she's got like, a *nine-day* layover, and wants to spend every second of it with you. You make

47 They say stress is the silent killer. But poison darts are also pretty damn quiet.

48 If you happened to be reading that sentence when you got neck-darted.

49 Mainly because your pants cost more than his house.

excuses for the first three or four days—during which you basically have to keep your phone plugged into the charger because she's calling and texting you every waking minute—but by day five she's really starting to get pouty.

You realize that at some point in the future you will probably have another mission to whatever grim, diesel-choked shithole she's from, and that you will definitely want some female companionship while you're there. Either her or maybe that big, blowzy friend of hers who was working coach. So you take her out to a just-okay restaurant, get some drinks down her gullet (and she's not only Eastern European but also a stewardess, so be prepared to buy it by the *liter*), and work the conversation around to asking if she would maybe, possibly—and not necessarily tonight, but not necessarily *not* tonight—be open to a threesome with her big, blowzy friend.

And guess what?

She totally is. Turns out they both are. They do it all the time, as a matter of fact.

You snap your fingers for the check as she makes a phone call. You literally whip the cab driver like a horse to make him drive faster. You get to your place just as Big Blowzy does, and before you know it, all three of you are covered in champagne and grape-seed oil and feathers, and blasting from your stereo—at that very moment—is none other than Bell Biv DeVoe's "Poison."

And then you die.

From whatever was on that umbrella. *A week ago*. Which is why I have spent the past decade building up an immunity to the seven poisons most commonly used in my line of work, by injecting myself with trace amounts of them. I *highly* disrecommend trying this yourself. You shouldn't even mess around with mushrooms unless you're a board-certified mycologist.[50] For reasons of national (not to mention personal) security, I obviously cannot share with you what these seven poisons are, but my mnemonic device for remembering them is CAPGURF.[51]

And so, in summation: poison sucks. Mostly because there's nothing you can realistically do to safeguard against it. Not unlike sexually transmitted diseases. Or unwanted pregnancies.

POISON BY THE NUMBERS

- Number of poisons to which I am (probably, hopefully) immune: 7
- Milliliters of poison from the *Phyllobates terribilis* it takes to kill a grown man: 0.03
- Rank of Bell Biv DeVoe's Poison on the U.S. Billboard Hot 100 chart: 3
- Telephone number for the Poison Control Center (U.S. only): 800-222-1222
- Times cooler this book would have been with a chapter about cobras: 50

50 Or possibly some sort of wood-elf.

51 Although, if you are a poisoner, that was probably too revealing.

CASINOS

For reasons unbeknownst to me, an inordinate amount of international espionage is centered around casinos. I would like to believe it's because secret agents—and the women who love them—live incredibly exciting lives and thus thrill at the idea of fortunes, both great and small, being won or lost on the turn of a single card. I would absolutely like to believe that.

But the truth is, it's much more likely because the type of person who is attracted to a career in the clandestine services to begin with—slightly arrogant, somewhat shallow, hypersexual high-functioning alcoholics with incredibly addictive personalities[52]—is really just there for the glamorous

52 The results of my own personal Myers-Briggs Type Indicator test were actually forwarded to Interpol.

ambience, the top-shelf booze, and the world-class hookers.

Because we're not talking Biloxi or Tunica here, guys. We're not even talking Vegas. We're talking Monaco.[53] And I don't know what Prince Rainier was thinking about, because those Monegasque hookers (*of which he had his pick!*) make Grace Kelly look like Alex Karras.

But, as with many things, there is a price to be paid for such beauty. And the last time I was there, that price was hovering right around $12,000 USD. And while that's for an overnight outcall, and both GFE and Greek are usually understood—by both parties—to be included in that price, and also these hookers are in fact the most beautiful women in the world, that's still pretty steep. Because while I have (obviously) paid for it, I sure as hell haven't ever overpaid.

I'll get to how I avoid being overcharged for sex in a moment, but first let me clarify one thing about the gaming industry for you: Look around. See that opulent casino you're standing in? Feel how thick that carpet is? See that inlaid Brazilian rosewood on the roulette wheel? Remember the perfect weave on the doorman's gabardine topcoat? See those hot-ass hookers?

Now guess how the casino paid for all that. If your answer was "by floating a tax-exempt municipal bond," you would be

---

53 And, more specifically, Monte Carlo. Which is in Monaco. The capital of which is *also* called Monaco. Which can be pretty confusing. The point is, the hookers are crazy-hot. And here's a thing you probably didn't know about Monaco: it's a sovereign nation. Like most non-Monegasques, you probably just thought it was a part of France. But Monaco has its own constitution, royal family, palace, the works. Monaco does rely on France for military protection, however (which is sort of like the United States relying on Mexico to build our cars for us), but Monaco's only other even slightly feasible military option would be Italy, with which Monaco is non-contiguous. Plus it's not like the Italians are any great prize militarily. I mean, Italy just barely squeaked one out over *Ethiopia,* for fuck's sake.

incorrect. A private corporation can't even do that. Which is why the casino paid for all that stuff with money from idiots like you, who walk in there and turn out their pockets every minute of their dumb lives.

"But Archer," you say, stupidly, "the whole time I'm in there, I'm getting free drinks!"

Well, actually you just drank nine watery, orange-juice-concentrate screwdrivers and paid a couple hundred bucks for the privilege. And guess what, genius: for less than a Jackson you could buy so much grain alcohol that, if you drank it all at once, you would literally *die*.

"But Archer," you say, stupidlier, "I gamble for the excitement, for the thrill of it all!"

Congratulations: you're stupid. Because there's nothing thrilling about a predetermined outcome. And the outcome of any game in any casino in any country in the world has already been predetermined (by Harvard computer geniuses using complex computer algorithms, who, having completed their task, were then murdered and dissolved in drums of acid by the Mafia). Check out the odds on any casino game. Are they one to one? No, they're not. Which means that if you play long enough, you're going to lose all your money. After which you will then probably end up blowing that well-dressed doorman for a five-dollar chip. Which you will immediately go gamble away. Like the pathetic, dick-breathed, nickel-slots junky you have become.

Which is why I don't gamble.

Because it's not gambling if you have a foolproof system![54] Which I do! And which I can't believe I'm sharing with you people, but it kills me to think of you dopes stuffing your hard-earned Hamiltons into the pockets of some mobster's silk-lined Brioni suit.

---

54 True story: one time I'm driving through the desert, about an hour outside of Vegas. It's at *least* 120 degrees. I get flagged down by this Chinese guy, who's kinda staggering around by the side of the road with his shirt wrapped around his head. I give him a ride and one of eight gallons of water I had in the trunk (because this is the desert, and I'm not an idiot) and he tells me that he has just lost all his money in Vegas. And he's like, utterly dumbfounded that this happened, because he has a "foolproof system." Which, it turns out, was this: Sit down at the roulette table. Pick a number. Keep betting that same number, over and over and over and over again, until it hits. *And then let it ride.* In the hopes that the same number will hit *twice in a row.* Seriously. And I never found out how or why he had gotten so far out into that sun-blasted desert, but this is my favorite part: he was walking back *toward* Vegas.

And so here, for the first time ever, is a step-by-step guide to the Sterling Archer Triple-A Power Play[55]:

1. Get $100,000 from somewhere.
2. Deposit it with the casino.
3. Have a drink with the charming personal concierge the casino will assign to you. Let him know you're interested in some female companionship after you have dinner and take in a show. (Note: If your personal concierge is a woman, this is a good time to bang her. And then let her know you're interested in some *different* female companionship after you have dinner and take in a show. Regardless of the gender of your personal concierge, this is also a good time to mention any food allergies you may have: he or she will be sure to let the chef know.)
4. Invite your personal concierge up to your comped suite, which is so mind-blowingly awesome that Frank fucking Sinatra would be nervous about walking around in there with his shoes on. The reason for doing this is so your personal concierge can use his own money to tip the bellhop. Just pat your pockets and look momentarily horrified, and the concierge will leap at the chance to do you this small kindness, as he is expecting a *huge* tip on the back end. (Oh, and if your personal concierge is a woman, this is a good opportunity to bang her again.)

55 The Triple-A stands for "Awesome Awesome Awesome."

5. Dismiss everyone and walk over to the bar by your suite's floor-to-ceiling windows and, as you watch the setting sun bathe the desert in hues of cinnamon and gold, start pounding the shit out of that free high-end liquor. Go nuts: Make a Long Island Iced Tea with sixty-year-old Armagnac. Then throw it on the floor; it's gross. Then call housekeeping. Then strip naked.
6. When the maid knocks, just yell for her to come on in. She may be startled by your nudity, but just offer her a drink while reassuring her that everything is, in fact, totally cool.[56] Then ask her if she'd like to have sex. If you look like I do naked, then yes, yes she would.
7. Have sex with the maid. Then, as you head to the bathroom, politely remind her about all that sticky broken glass over by the bar. (Note: It is *not* acceptable to offer her money. This will make her feel like a whore, and she's probably incredibly Catholic. It *is* acceptable to offer her five or six bottles of the casino's high-end liquor. This avoids any appearance of impropriety, plus she'll be able to trade it for tortilla flour, cooking oil, and safety matches.)

56 *"No no no, todo está bien, linda, todo está bien. ¿Bebida?"*

8. Shower, take a short nap, and get dressed for the evening.
9. Have an amazing, and totally comped, dinner in the casino's VIP restaurant. Then order an entirely *separate* meal, which you will instruct your waiter to have delivered to that cinnamon-skinned maid, down in whatever steamy sub-basement laundry room she's currently toiling. The waiter will recognize this for the totally class move it is, and comp this second dinner as well.
10. Take in a show. I prefer magicians, but I'm also pretty crazy about endangered species. Luckily this is Vegas (oh, yeah, I forgot: this is Vegas), and you can't swing a dead hooker without hitting some magic act built almost entirely around the majestic white Bengal Tiger.
11. Head back to the casino. At this point, your personal concierge will inquire, very politely, if you're ready to try your luck at the tables. Tell him that you're dying to gamble, but that you don't think you could concentrate until you blow a few hot, salty loads all over at least two top-tier prostitutes. Definitely comped, preferably while tearing through the desert in the back of a comped stretch limousine with the stereo blasting Led Zeppelin's "When the Levee Breaks."
12. Go do that.
13. Now comes the tricky part, because you've gotten yourself into a bit of a corner here. Your personal concierge has satisfied his part of the implied oral agreement: at this very minute, two sexy hookers have one foot up on a sink in the lobby bathroom and are using lemon-scented moist towelettes to wipe your seed from their various female nooks and/or crannies. He is—and rightfully so, I might add—expecting you to walk over

to the cage, withdraw a stack of those cool, black, rectangle-y chips, and then go sit down at a table and gamble them away. And while *he's* being incredibly polite about it, his Mafia colleagues probably won't be. So:

14. Go get your chips, bitch: it's time to gamble. Now, I'm personally attracted to the games with the most paraphernalia: roulette, pachinko, or anything with a light-up tote-board. If I gambled, and if a casino would let me, I could probably spend hours happily betting on the board game *Mouse Trap*. But since I don't, and they won't, and I'm just trying to get the hell out of here with my money and my thumbs, I head for the pai gow tables. These are usually pretty easy to spot: just look for the cloud of cigarette smoke that doesn't speak English. You will be the only white person at the table, and you may get a few dirty looks when you sit down, but that's just because Asians can be kinda racist sometimes. Wave to (or snap your fingers at) a waitress and tell her to bring a bottle of Johnnie Walker Black *for the table*. Hey, look who just made a bunch of new friends! Gesture toward the tabletop and shrug, like you don't understand how the game is played. Then start pouring shots of scotch for all those guys—and a woman you wouldn't be at all surprised to learn is Madame Chiang Kai-Shek—as they try to explain the rules by jabbering nonsense at you, waving their cigarettes around, and quickly getting bombed on scotch (remember: they're *tiny*). Just keep playing dumb, order another bottle, and don't be alarmed if everybody's face turns bright red: they're not mad at you. This condition is called Oriental Flush, and it happens to some Asian people when they drink. Off-putting, but harmless. Okay, once everybody is totally shitfaced (which should probably

take about eight minutes), throw your hands up like you're just too dumb to ever learn the subtle nuances of pai gow (which you probably are). Then indicate, with lots of pointing and tummy-rubbing, that you'd like to take them all out to dinner. (Note: getting Asian people to voluntarily walk away from any type of gambling is obviously going to be a tough sell, but don't take no for an answer: this next bit is the crucial part of The Sterling Archer Triple-A Power Play.) Shepherd the whole drunken, red-faced, smoking, shouting lot of them over to the cage and tell the cashier you wish to cash out your chips. Your personal concierge will come *sprinting* over to the cage at this point—trying to catch the eye of a few Mafia goons as he does so—and ask how he may be of assistance. You'll both have to shout over your drunken little herd of Asians because now they're arguing about where to eat and are thus louder and angrier sounding than normal. Tell him you're taking your new friends out to dinner, and that you don't feel comfortable leaving a hundred thousand dollars in the casino vault. He knows—hell, even Madame Chiang Kai-Shek knows—that this is complete bullshit, because it was sitting there the whole time you were out scarfing down Lobster Thermidor and pressure-washing hookers and watching tigers magically disappear. But the shouting, arm-waving, beet-faced Asians (who appear to have agreed on barbecue) will have him so flummoxed that you'll be able to withdraw your hundred grand, go eat a bunch of short ribs with the gang, and be in a cab to McCarran before he realizes what the hell just happened.

15. Rinse.[57]
16. Repeat.[58]

And there you have it: the Sterling Archer Triple-A Power Play.[59]

ARCHER FUN FACT: ROULETTE

Here's a fun fact: Add up all the numbers on a roulette wheel, one through thirty-six. Go ahead, I'll wait. Are you adding the last number right now? What did you get? Creepy, right?

ARCHER BY THE NUMBERS: CASINO ODDS

- Odds against being dealt a royal flush in poker: 649,740:1
- Odds against making a "Hard Eight" in craps: 10:1
- Odds against getting a 00 in roulette: 35:1
- Odds for seeing some Asian people there: 1:1
- Odds for those Asians smoking: 1:1
- Toll-free gambling addiction hotline: 800-522-4700

---

[57] And you are going to want to rinse, because you didn't wear a condom with those hookers. But don't worry about it: they're probably on the Pill. (Plus you told them your name was Elvis Roosevelt.)

[58] At some other casino, because come within a half-mile of this one again and you're going to be *walking* to the airport. Mainly because no cabbie in the world is going to pick up a guy whose balls have been stuffed into his mouth.

[59] While many things (Spanish-speaking housekeepers, magical tigers, etc.) in this particular scenario may seem applicable only to Las Vegas, the shouting, tomato-faced Asian herd is not: walk into any casino in any country in the world, and you will see some Asians smoking and scowling and playing the absolute shit out of some pai gow.

SURVEILLANCE

Wow. I kinda shot my wad with the Sterling Archer Triple-A Power Play. Not sure if I'm in the mood to get into a whole big thing about how binoculars work.

INTERROGATION

In today's political climate, "interrogation" has been become a very sensitive issue. And I put it in quotation marks because, by now, even tiny little kids know that "interrogation" is just grown-up talk for torture. But in my opinion, we're doing our children a grave disservice by refusing to engage in an open dialogue about torture. Which is the same thing we do with sex. And then the next thing those kids know, they're of barely legal age and someone is trying to put his penis in them, and they're all like, "What the *fuck*, dude?! Jesus, hang *on* a second! What? No, I'm not *mad*, I just wasn't expecting that, because my parents never engaged in an open dialogue with me about it. But let's do a bong hit, and you can maybe walk me through it."

And that's your *child*. I mean, obviously they're not still a child when they get brusquely introduced to sex by a stranger they just met in a bar like, an hour ago; they're a young adult. A young adult with his or her underpants around his or her ankles, hunched over a bong in the back of this guy's pick-up, and the only even remotely non-appalling thing about the whole situation is the truck has a camper top, the windows of which are illegally—yet mercifully—over-tinted. Because there is a *grammar* school right across the *street*, for God's sake.

Hang on—I lost my thread a little bit. What are we doing? Oh, right. Torture. Yes.

Torture is one of those things that Americans constantly whine about (e.g., the inhumane treatment of cows), but then they go out and exhibit the exact behavior (e.g., gobbling down a big platter of delicious sliders) that perpetuates the necessity of that thing in the first place.

Americans are repelled by the very thought of their government's sanctioning torture, and yet they demand to not be blown up by terrorists. But it's the exact same principle. Except that the cows are now terrorists—a chilling thought in and of itself—and national security is now a steaming plate of hot, juicy miniburgers. And you can't have your sliders and eat 'em too, folks.

Also, they don't actually torture the cows: they just pack them in feedlots, knee-deep in their own excrement, until it's time to blow a hole in their foreheads with a pneumatic bolt, slam a big steel hook into their hind leg, yank them up into the air, slice them into various steaks, chops, ribs, butts, and rounds, and then macerate whatever's left over into ground chuck, which is then formed into delicious little patties, grilled with a bit of Vidalia onion and topped with a small slice of cheese and a bread-and-butter pickle, slipped into a tiny steamed bun, and then carried to your table by a smiling, apple-cheeked waitress who's working her way through college so that one day, God willing, she can become a veterinarian. And thus continues the circle of life.

My point is, I personally don't torture people.[60]

60 We job that out.

INTERROGATION RESISTANCE

The key to resisting interrogation techniques is, as with many things, *mental preparation*.

Because have you ever broken a fingernail, way down past the quick? Or gotten an electric shock while using two forks to get a pre-buttered English muffin out of the toaster? Or stubbed your pinky toe *really* badly on the metal leg of your bed frame?[61]

Great. Now imagine a guy using a pair of Vise-Grips to actually pull your fingernails *out*, one at a time. Then imagine being stripped naked, lashed to a set of metal bedsprings, doused with water, and that same guy running a set of jumper cables from a 4000-watt generator directly to your testicles. Then imagine a second guy—the first guy, having just lit a cigarette off your still-smoldering scrotum, is taking a smoke break—using a ball-peen hammer to smash each and every one of your toes into amorphous, pulpy little bloblets.

And those are just things I made up just now. I don't torture people for a living. But torturers do—hence the name—and they have *countless* ways of inflicting the most unimaginable

61 You strike me as the sort of person whose bed would be on a cheap metal frame.

pain that you could ever possibly imagine. If it were even imaginable. So I don't care who you are, sooner or later you're going to tell your torturers *everything* they want to know, whether it's true or not. And when you do, you won't care that you're betraying your friends and colleagues and countrymen. Because you'll be too busy trying not to look at—with your one remaining eyeball—your other, non-remaining eyeball. Which is staring up at you from the gore-spattered floor.

You are going to talk.

And your torturer—if he's good at his job, which he probably is; there's probably tons of competition—will make this very clear to you at the very beginning. As he removes his woolen tunic, rolls up his shirtsleeves, and hands the assistant torturer his wristwatch:

You are going to talk.

He will repeat this fact a few moments later. As he lays all the various and horrifying tools of his black trade on a rolling cart built for the express purpose of torture-tool-holding:

You are going to talk.

He will repeat this fact a few moments later. As he lights a cigarette with a hammer-and-sickle-embossed Zippo. Which he then snaps shut for dramatic effect and tells you, once again:

You. Are going. To talk.

And he is absolutely right. So why go through all that blinding, soul-destroying pain from which you will never recover—physically, let alone mentally—when you're just going to blab your head off anyway? Just go ahead and tell him whatever the hell he wants to know. *Now*, before he slides a rectal thermometer up your urethra and smashes your dick with a tire iron, filling your now-ruined penis with a thousand tiny shards of glass and a shitload of mercury.

Because *now* is when that *mental preparation* will prove itself so invaluable. Because if your torturers don't shoot you in the back of the skull when it's over (which they probably will, which is even less reason to sweat all this stuff), you're going to have to deal with a *ton* of guilt for being responsible for the deaths of so many of your friends and colleagues and countrymen. But because you have *mentally prepared* yourself for the weight of this crushing guilt, you will be able to walk out of that torture chamber with your head held high. You will walk out like a man.

Because your testicles are still attached your body.

ESCAPE AND EVASION

Given the overall tone of my writing style, this may sound like I'm just being a dick:

Don't get caught.

But it's actually the first thing they tell you at the ISIS Escape and Evasion seminar. And it's actually very sound advice: it is much, much easier to *avoid* capture than to escape once you *are* captured. And even though you planned ahead and inserted a tactical suppository into your pre-buttered rectum, in all likelihood, you won't be able to rely on it. Because thirty seconds into your first torture session (see above), you're probably going to fear-poop it out.

But sometimes, often through no real fault of his own, an intelligence agent simply cannot avoid capture. Strong winds may cause his parachute jump to miss his drop zone, for example. The smallest mistake in a regional accent of a foreign language, or perhaps even a tiny detail in the exquisite cut of his suit, may betray the agent's true identity to an alert and well-trained enemy agent. Or he might just blab it out when he's drunk in a bar somewhere.

The point is far better men than you have been exposed, captured, tortured, and summarily executed in a damp cellar by a fat, drunken NKVD noncom, whose bonus for putting a 7.62mm slug into their brain stem was a liter of lukewarm potato vodka. Far, far better men.

So if you are captured, try not to beat yourself up. Someone else will do it for you.

Oh, and no matter what anyone tells you, do *not* bury your parachute at the drop zone. Because—especially if you've parachuted behind the Iron Curtain, where even mundane items like soap or hot cabbage can be a luxury—do you have any idea how laid you can get with eighty yards of *silk*?

DID YOU KNOW . . . ?

That the arteries of a blue whale are so large that a leopard can crawl through them?

WILDERNESS SURVIVAL

The topic of wilderness survival could probably be a book unto itself. In fact, I bet it already has been. And since I pretty generally get to pick my assignments, and since I pretty generally pick assignments which require me to go somewhere non-wildernessy like Monte Carlo or Gstaad or the Netherlands Antilles, which means I pretty generally don't spend a ton of time in the wilderness, why don't we just leave this topic to one of those books? I'm sure anything with "wilderness" or "survival" or any combination of those two words in the title will be perfectly fine for what you're trying to do. Which is apparently starve to death in a forest.

COBRAS

[THIS PAGE INTENTIONALLY LEFT BLANK][62]

62 Through no fault of the author's.

SECTION TWO

HOW TO
DRINK

First and foremost, before we continue I'd like to make one thing perfectly clear: A martini is made with gin. If your martini is made with vodka, it is not, in fact, a martini. And odds are that you have a vagina.

There. Now we can move on. To the drinking. Of which many of you readers may think that I do too much. And I can't honestly say that opinion is entirely unfair. But what many people fail to consider is that a large part of my drinking is done professionally, not socially. It's a very real, very important part of my job description. (As the world's greatest secret agent.)

Because I never know, for example, when I'll be required to down shot after shot of pepper vodka with a smoke-and-body-odor-filled roomful of KGB agents while also remembering that I'm supposed to be speaking Russian.[63] And so yes, I drink a lot. But only because I need to keep my alcohol tolerance at the highest level humanly possible.

And also because I'm pretty sure if I stopped drinking for even one day, the accumulated hangover would probably kill me.

And with that sobering thought in mind—if you will excuse the pun, in what up until now has been an incredible, if not life-changing, read—here's a list of my favorite cocktail recipes.[64]

63 Which, by the way, isn't my strongest foreign language to begin with. I'm not actually all that great in *any* foreign language. Although this is much less of a handicap for a secret agent than you might imagine because, in my considerable experience, people in foreign countries always just speak English, just with a heavy accent of whatever country they're supposed to be from. So international travel is pretty much like watching *Hogan's Heroes*.

64 Also in alphabetical order, turns out. Apparently my editrix is

COCKTAIL RECIPES

Please note that the following are *cocktail* recipes. You won't find anything about wine in this section because, not to belabor the point, I don't have a vagina.

I mean, yes, obviously, I will drink wine if somebody hands me a glass full of it. Red, white, rosé, even the lowly white Zinfandel: it doesn't matter, I will drink it. Sparkling wine: champagne, cava, or prosecco—yes, any and all that I can get my hands on. Sweet wine: no joke, a lot of times for lunch I will just go sit on a bench somewhere and drink an entire bottle of port.

I also didn't include *highball* recipes, because a highball is technically just spirits and a mixer. And if you need a recipe for a scotch and soda, you probably shouldn't be drinking anyway, because you're severely developmentally disabled. And think these words are ants.

I also didn't include recipes for my favorite *unmixed drinks*—I'm a pretty big fan of neat bourbon and scotch, for example—because even though by this point I'm really just trying to pad the word count, for those drinks you just pour them into a glass. Or your mouth. Or a high-heeled shoe. Or a woman's navel. Or your navel. Really, the only limit is your imagination.

A final note about cocktails: You probably assume it's

important to use only the highest-quality spirits. In this assumption you would be absolutely correct. But it is *equally* important to use only the highest-quality mixers, ingredients, and assorted garnishes. Why use a thirty-year-old Garrafeira porto for a Porto flip, and then mix it with a nonorganic, non-cage-free egg yolk?

A (second) final note about cocktails: If at all possible, avoid mixing your own. It sends the wrong message. Because there's usually somebody standing there who should be doing it for you: bartender, valet, midlevel diplomat, a woman, etc.

Bellini

I refuse to include a recipe for the Bellini. If you want a Bellini, go to Harry's Bar in Venice and order a Bellini. Because that's the only place on earth you should ever drink one.

Bloody Mary

A fitting way to start the cocktail section in earnest, as this is generally the way I start my day: in earnest. Packed with the vitamins and minerals I need to make it through a strenuous day of secret agenting, plus plenty of vodka (which I just want), the Bloody is the cornerstone upon which Woodhouse builds my sumptuous breakfasts. Variations abound, but this is my favorite:

3 ounces vodka
6 ounces freshly squeezed tomato juice
1 ounce freshly squeezed key lime juice
½ teaspoon freshly grated horseradish
Dash of Worcestershire sauce
Dash of hot sauce
Dash of salt and pepper

Shake ingredients, over ice, in a cocktail mixer. Pour mixture and ice into an imperial pint glass and garnish, using one of those cool little plastic swords they have, with:

1 rib organic celery, with leafy bits still attached
3 Extremedura olives (pitted and pimiento-ed ahead of time by your valet)
3 caper berries

Note: For a Bloody Caesar, simply replace the tomato juice with 6 ounces of Clamato. You will not be sorry.)

Brandy Alexander

Invented in 334 BC by the imperial mixologist to Alexander the Great, to celebrate his (Alexander's) victory over the Persians. Who I think are now the Iranians. But also, who cares?

2 ounces cognac
2 ounces crème de cacao
2 ounces half-and-half (or heavy cream, if you're Pam)
Pinch of nutmeg

Shake ingredients, over ice, in a cocktail mixer. Strain into a chilled cocktail glass. Garnish with nutmeg.[65]

---

65 Malcolm X used to get high on nutmeg to kick his heroin habit when he got sent to prison for burglary before he became a movie star (which is pretty cool). Two tablespoons of nutmeg will kill you (which isn't).

Caipirinha

I love everything about Brazil. Like, I don't mean to sound unpatriotic, but I really wish the Brazilians would get their shit together and conquer the entire world. Enslave me, already.

½ lime, cut into wedges
2 teaspoons crystal sugar
2 ounces cachaça

With a wooden muddler (which please tell me you have), muddle lime and sugar in an old-fashioned glass. Fill glass with crushed ice and add cachaça. Some bartenders will insist on garnishing your caipirinha with a piece of sugar cane, but to me that's just empty calories.

Cuba Libre

A Cuba Libre is just a rum and cola with a lime. I never order this from a male bartender, because if I ask for a Cuba Libre, they give me a shitty look. But if I ask for a rum and cola with a lime, they always snark back with "You mean a Cuba Libre?" To which I reply "No, I mean, what's it like working for the minimum server wage, which is actually far lower than the regular minimum wage? I mean I know you get tips, but still . . . I'd eat a shotgun."

2 ounces dark rum
4 ounces cola
1 lime wedge, as garnish

Pour the rum and cola over ice. Garnish with the lime wedge.[66]

66 Today. Dumbass.

Daiquiri

Invented in Havana's El Floridita bar and made famous by Ernest Hemingway, winner of both the Pulitzer Prize in Fiction and the Nobel Prize for Literature.[67] Hey, Papa: now we've both written a book.

4 ounces white rum
2 ounces freshly squeezed key lime juice
½ ounce gomme syrup[68]

Shake ingredients, over ice, in a cocktail mixer. Strain into a chilled cocktail glass.

French 75

Invented in 1915 at Harry's New York Bar. Which turns out is actually in Paris (France).

2 ounces gin
1 ounce gomme syrup[69]
1 ounce freshly squeezed lemon juice
Brut champagne (for which cava or prosecco may be freely substituted), to top up
1 lemon twist, as garnish

Shake first three ingredients, over ice, in a cocktail mixer. Strain into an ice-filled Collins glass and top up with champagne (or dry sparkling wine of your choosing; it's your house). Garnish with twist.

---

67 I realize that it's in fairly poor taste to have an entry concerning Ernest Hemingway immediately follow a joke about eating a shotgun. Take it up with my alphabetically anal editrix.

68 I don't know what this is, and Woodhouse is out running errands.

69 Woodhouse still isn't back yet.

ARCHER FUN FACT: ERNEST HEMINGWAY

Most of the cool guys from back in Hemingway's time—John Huston, David Niven, Clark Gable, Eric Sevareid, Winston Churchill, etc.—thought Hemingway was a dick.

Gibson

A joyless drink for dour, low-level, consular functionaries, the Gibson is simply a martini (see page 81) in which a pearl onion shamelessly attempts to replace the olive. As if it ever could.

Gimlet

The original gin and juice. Invented by pirates in the eleventh century to prevent scurvy and, presumably, to help mentally prepare them for all the raping they were going to be doing later. Originally served neat (because pirates didn't have ice, duh) it can also be served on the rocks.

4 ounces gin[70]
½ ounce freshly squeezed lime juice
½ ounce Rose's lime juice
1 lime wedge, as garnish

Shake liquid ingredients, over ice, in a cocktail mixer. Strain

---

70 You may notice it says "gin" and not "gin *or* vodka." That's because this is a recipe for a gimlet, and not a "vodka gimlet," which—regardless of what anyone tells you—simply does not exist. The cocktail of which you're thinking is properly referred to as a "vodka, combined with the ingredients that any sane person would use to make a gimlet."

into a chilled cocktail glass or, if you are not a pirate, over ice in an old-fashioned glass. Garnish with the lime wedge.

Green Russian

This is the only time in this entire cocktail section that I'll say this: be careful with these.

- 2 ounces absinthe
- 2 ounces vodka
- 1 ounce crème de menthe
- 2 ounces milk (Pam, being a lost cause, uses heavy cream)

Shake ingredients, over ice, in a cocktail mixer. Strain into an ice-filled collins glass. Drink, while thinking about the decisions that have brought you to this very spot, at this very moment.

Gummi Roy

A Rob Roy is basically a Manhattan in which the whiskey is replaced with scotch. A Gummi Roy is basically a Rob Roy in which the sweet vermouth is replaced with gummi bears.

- 5 gummi bears
- 2 ounces scotch

Place gummi bears in a rocks glass. Add scotch. A child could do it. In fact, the brightly-colored, kid-friendly gummi bears make this an excellent drink to teach children about cocktails.

Long Island Iced Tea

There are very, very few good things that have come from Long Island. Yeah, no, I can't actually think of a single other thing besides this cocktail. An excellent drink to serve a female companion, although prudence dictates you know her body weight within a margin of error of three pounds. Actually, prudence dictates you know this no matter what you're serving her.

1 ounce vodka
1 ounce gin
1 ounce white rum
1 ounce triple sec
1 ounce tequila (seriously, this drink doesn't fuck around)
2 ounces freshly squeezed lemon juice
2 ounces gomme syrup[71]
Splash of cola
1 lemon slice, as garnish

Shake ingredients, over ice, in a cocktail mixer. Strain into pint glass filled with ice, garnish with the lemon slice. Hand someone your keys. House keys, too: you can just smash in a window.

Mai Tai

Tropical and delicious but, like the Bellini, unless you're drinking it at the source (the original Don the Beachcomber's in Los Angeles, now closed), there's really no point in trying.

---

71 Still not back.

Manhattan

One of several delicious cocktails named after a place. Also, the cherry makes it a nice late-morning transitional cocktail, to help ease you into whatever you'll be drinking at lunch.

- 2½ ounces rye or Canadian whiskey
- 1 ounce sweet red vermouth
- 1 dash angostura bitters (although Peychaud's is entirely acceptable)
- 1 maraschino[72] cherry, as garnish

Shake ingredients, over ice, in a cocktail mixer. Strain into a chilled cocktail glass and garnish with the maraschino cherry. Sip, while thinking about how cool you are. Yeah, you're doing okay.

Martini

I think I've made my stance on acceptable martini ingredients pretty clear. Although, in a certain other (lame British) secret agent's defense, I do have to admit that the earliest version of his so-called "martini" was actually fairly non-vaginal, as it contained both gin *and* vodka *and* a great big shot of Lillet Blonde. And also a slice of lemon peel, which, whatever, but two or three of those bastards, and your liver will definitely know that you're expecting great things from it.

However, I think I've also made it pretty clear that I don't like to invite comparison to He-Who-Must-Not-Be-Named. And so here is *Sterling Archer*'s recipe for a *martini*. Deal.

---

[72] Which is pronounced *mar-a-SKEE-no*. And even money says you're also mispronouncing bruschetta. Dummy.

5 ounces gin
1 ounce dry vermouth
1 tablespoon Extremedura olive juice
3 Extremedura olives as garnish
(pitted and pimento-ed ahead of time by your valet)[73]

Pour gin, vermouth, olive juice, and ice cubes into a cocktail mixer and stir. (Just to be contrary; it makes no difference whether it's shaken or stirred, and only a colossal idiot believes otherwise.) Strain into a chilled cocktail glass. Garnish with olives speared on a tiny plastic sword. Sip, thinking about how it's actually pretty damn cool that you haven't become overexposed. Yet.

Mint Julep

Deceptively powerful. I once got so smashed on these at the Derby, I had sex with some huge-hatted married broad in a portable toilet. True story. Not a flattering story, just a true one.

4 to 7 fresh mint leaves
Granulated sugar, to taste
3 ounces bourbon

Muddle the mint, sugar, and a small amount of crushed ice in an old-fashioned glass. Add the bourbon and top it off with crushed ice. Garnish with a sprig of mint and serve in a silver julep cup. Or, hey, you know what? While you're at it, just make two and dump it all into a plastic cup: twenty minutes from now, you're gonna be destroying someone's marriage in a fiberglass shithouse.

---

73 Which I'm pretty sure You-Know-Who doesn't have.

ARCHER FUN FACT: BOURBON

Contrary to popular belief, bourbon whiskey may be produced anywhere in the United States, and not exclusively in Kentucky. Same thing goes for banging your cousin.

Mojito

Somebody please remind me: Why is it we don't like Cuba? Seriously, did I miss something? Did John F. Kennedy walk into the Oval Office one day, only to find Fidel Castro lighting his Cohiba with the American flag while teabagging Jackie? In front of John-John? What? Oh, communism. Oh, okay, now I get . . . No, that still doesn't make sense. Seriously?

3 sprigs fresh mint, plus more to garnish
2 teaspoons granulated sugar
1½ ounces freshly squeezed lime juice
2 ounces white rum
Soda water, to top up

Muddle the mint, sugar, and lime juice in a collins glass. Fill the glass with crushed ice. Add the rum and top it up with soda water. Garnish with a sprig of mint and serve with a straw. Sip, thinking about how awesome it would be if the Bay of Pigs Invasion had worked and we were all down there right now, up to our eyeballs in the hottest, roundest, mochaccino-coloredest asses on the planet.

Molotov Cocktail

I guess this technically doesn't belong in this section. For one thing, since it contains fewer than three ingredients, the Molotov cannot correctly be called a cocktail. For another thing, it's an incendiary device which, if you live in the United States, is specifically prohibited under the National Firearms Act. So unless you happen to live in Finland sometime between 1940 and 1945, not only do not drink this, please please please do not even attempt to make it.[74]

1 750 ml glass bottle
(if you're an adult; kids may want
to use a 250 ml or 500 ml bottle)
750 ml gasoline (or however many milliliters
you ended up going with, bottle-wise)
1 foot duct tape, torn in half lengthwise
4 storm matches

Live in Finland between 1940 and 1945. Fill bottle with gasoline. Replace cap. Use duct tape to secure matches, longitudinally, to the side of the bottle. Go find some Soviet (or, later, Nazi) invaders driving around your little Finnish village in a half-track. Light matches and throw cocktail at the Soviet (or, later, Nazi) half-track. Hide. Await swift and appallingly brutal reprisal.

---

74 Seriously. HarperCollins is far enough up my ass already.

Moscow Mule

I was worried that, given the overall espionage theme of this book, the Moscow Mule might seem like too obvious a choice. But then I realized go write your own fucking book.

2 ounces vodka
2 ounces freshly squeezed lime juice
5 ounces ginger beer

Shake ingredients, over ice, in a cocktail mixer. Strain into an ice-filled old-fashioned glass.

Negroni

One of several Italian exports which, like the Vespa or the Fiat 500, should only be driven by a woman. Although apparently frozen-pea-spokesperson Orson Welles was a big fan.

1½ ounces gin
1½ ounces sweet red vermouth
1½ ounces Campari
1 slice orange peel, as garnish

Mix ingredients and serve, over ice, in an old-fashioned glass. Garnish with orange peel.

Peppermint Patty

Another kid-friendly cocktail. And just *amazing* with a toasty raclette, back at the lodge after a cold day on the slopes in Gstaad. Or on a bearskin rug with a beautiful woman, as you both bask in post-coital bliss and the warming glow of a crackling fire. Ooh, or on a hayride!

12 ounces prepared hot cocoa
(Scratch-made, not instant; I shouldn't have to say that.)
8 ounces peppermint schnapps
Mini-marshmallows (optional), as garnish

Combine schnapps and hot cocoa in a thermos. Garnish with mini-marshmallows, if desired.

Pimm's Cup

At first glance, this drink seems like the Brits tried to do to cocktails what they have long done to food. And world wars. Seriously, is that a cucumber in your drink, or are you just glad to see Lend-Lease battleships steaming toward your Luftwaffe-pummeled shitbox of an island?

1 small English cucumber
3 ounces Pimm's No. 1
1 ounce freshly squeezed Meyer lemon juice
Pinch of sugar
Sprig of fresh rosemary
Sprig of thyme
Sprig of mint
1 slice Meyer lemon
1 fresh strawberry, halved
3 ounces carbonated lemonade *or* lemon-lime soda *or* ginger ale *or* ginger beer[75]

Cut two spears from the cucumber, set aside for garnish. Dice remaining cucumber and place it into a cocktail mixer. Muddle, then add Pimm's, lemon juice, sugar, and some ice.

---

75 Hi, welcome to England: we have no idea what we're supposed to be doing.

Shake vigorously and strain into an ice-filled Collins glass (or repurposed 40mm Luftwaffe shell casing). Add the herbs, lemon slice and strawberry halves. Fill the glass with carbonated lemonade (or whatever) and garnish with the cucumber spears. Think about all those brave Americans who died protecting a country that would invent a drink like this. Which, all kidding aside, is actually pretty delicious.

Pink Lady

The quintessential girly drink. Which doesn't mean that, not unlike a scorned stewardess, it can't embarrass the shit out of you in front of your current date and a restaurant full of people.

1½ ounces gin
½ ounce applejack
½ ounce freshly squeezed lemon juice
1 egg white
4 dashes grenadine
1 Maraschino cherry, to garnish

Shake all ingredients, plus ice but minus cherry, in a cocktail mixer. Strain into a chilled cocktail glass and garnish with cherry. Sip very slowly, while waiting for those guys down there at the other end of the bar to say a goddamn word.

Pisco Sour

Not to sound like a dick, but except for Paddington Bear (who is totally awesome!!!) Peru has never had much going for it. I mean, even the gruff-yet-loveable Paddington got out of there on the first train he could hop. But this cocktail goes a long way toward bolstering Peru's image.

2 ounces pisco
1 ounce freshly squeezed lime juice
¾ ounce simple syrup
1 egg white
Dash of angostura bitters
(although Peychaud's is acceptable)

Shake all ingredients, minus bitters, quite vigorously and over ice, in a cocktail mixer. Strain into a chilled cocktail glass and dash the bitters over the foam. Serve with a small marmalade sandwich.

Pruno

I'm making an exception here because pruno, being technically wine, does not belong in this section. But if you plan on becoming a secret agent, there's a good chance that at some point you'll find yourself imprisoned in some flyblown tropical shithole of a country. These countries are generally run by dictators who, among other things, are not known for their humane treatment of prisoners. So while you plot your escape (and subsequent revenge), you are definitely going to want to be shitfaced: the soles of your bastinado-ravaged feet will thank you.

1 vague amount of some type of citrus fruit
(although I've had luck with raisins)
1 small mound of sugar (turbinado is fine)
2 slices of bread
3 ketchup packets
(optional, and actually surprisingly hard to come by)
1 quart tap water
1 plastic bread bag

Force a weaker prisoner to combine all the ingredients in the plastic bread bag and store in the tank of the toilet in *his* cell, due to risk of random searches, for 14 days. Serve at room temperature in either a tin can or half a coconut shell. (Note: A gratuity of two cigarettes to your "pruno punk" is customary.)

Sidecar

Why doesn't anyone drink sidecars anymore? Or, for that matter, ride around in them? Because I can't think of a single thing I would rather do than get totally ripped on a thermos full of these babies while somebody motorcycles me around town and country in an actual sidecar.

2 ounces cognac
1 ounces Cointreau
1 ounce freshly squeezed lemon juice
1 lemon twist

Shake ingredients, over ice, in a cocktail mixer. Strain into chilled cocktail glass. (Some people prefer their sidecar served with a sugared rim, but those people have vaginas.)

Singapore Sling

Invented in the Long Bar of that timeless jewel of the Orient, the Raffles Hotel. From which I was banned after an entirely unfortunate altercation involving two prostitutes, a lemur, a rickshaw (and driver), and several members of the Singapore Police Force's Gurkha Contingent. And let me just say this about that: if you ever want to get the absolute shit kicked out of you—and want it done in a precise and professional manner—the Gurkhas are *the* shitkickers for you.

Anyway, it's lame the Raffles banned me, so I'm not including their stupid drink.

Sloe Gin Fizz

Chances are you've been misspelling this your entire life. I know I have. And now that I think about it, I actually will probably continue to do so. Because "phizz" just looks cooler to me.

3 ounces sloe gin
1 ounce freshly squeezed lemon juice
1 ounce gomme syrup[76]
5 ounces soda water

Shake gin, lemon juice, and the ever-elusive gomme syrup over ice, in a cocktail mixer. Strain into an ice-filled collins glass, then splash in the soda water to create a light and lovely phoam.

Tom Collins

There are very few people in this world whom I have a desire to meet. Mr. Collins, the creator of this refreshing and powerful libation, is one of them. He's probably dead, though.

3 ounces gin
3 ounces freshly squeezed lemon juice
1 teaspoon gomme syrup[77]
Soda water, to top up

[76] Seriously, how long does it take to pick up a bag of oranges?
[77] I am going to beat Woodhouse with that bag of oranges.

1 lemon slice, to garnish
1 maraschino cherry, to garnish

Fill a Collins[78] glass with ice. Add the gin, lemon juice, and the syrup your valet is going to wish he had prepared. Top up with soda water. Garnish with lemon slice and cherry, on a tiny sword.

Whiskey Sour

Oh my God. If I'd known that America had a gomme syrup–based economy, I would've invested in whatever stuff gomme syrup is made out of. I can't do that, however, because I obviously have no idea what that stuff is. The only thing I know is that Woodhouse is in trouble.

3 ounces bourbon
2 ounces freshly squeezed lemon juice
1 ounce gomme syrup[79]
1 orange slice, as garnish
1 maraschino cherry, to garnish

Shake ingredients, over ice, in a cocktail mixer. Strain into an ice-filled old-fashioned glass, the rim of which it is acceptable to sugar. Garnish with the orange slice and cherry, on a tiny sword.

Okay. Hopefully, that's enough to get you started.

---

78 Duh.

79 Seriously, thirty seconds after Woodhouse walks in the door with those oranges he will be bleeding internally.

SECTION THREE

HOW TO STYLE

This topic could *definitely* be an entire book unto itself. But it's also a topic that, since HarperCollins wasn't any too thrilled about the chapter on wilderness survival, I must now try to cram into *this* book. A book which, according to the word count silently mocking me from the lower left-hand corner of my computer screen, I have no idea how I'm ever going to finish.

Seriously, how do book authors do this? I doubt there's enough laudanum in the *world* to make this not suck. And there's definitely not enough in my penthouse.[80]

And so, in the interest of fulfilling my contractual obligations to (the ever-jealouser and increasingly more petulant man-haters at) HarperCollins, and because I may at some point run into you (though I can't possibly imagine where) and have to look at your clothes, I will now attempt to explain to you *how to* not walk around looking like a complete and utter dickbrain.

80 Woodhouse, the creaking old fiend, has some heroin stashed somewhere in here. But to be honest, I probably have enough addictions as it is. Also, I just assume it's hidden in his room somewhere, and the thought of even crossing the threshold of that foul little cell fills me with equal parts nausea and dread. Plus, I don't like needles.

VALETS

Before we begin, please allow me to define a few terms: a butler—sometimes referred to as a majordomo—is a male servant who oversees a large household staff. A valet—sometimes clumsily referred to as a gentleman's gentleman[81]—is the personal attendant to, as the latter phrase implies, a gentleman. It should be noted that *valet*, in the sense we will use it, rhymes with *mallet*. *Valet* rhymes with *ballet* only when referring to the sullen guy parking your car.[82]

I do not have a butler. I have a valet.

In my case, this valet is an embarrassingly ancient Englishman and heroin addict, who—no matter how loudly or longly I berate him for it—reeks of mothballs. And also whom—if he weren't personally responsible for seeing to my every waking, bathing, shaving, grooming, dressing, feeding, liquoring, re-feeding, re-liquoring, undressing, re-bathing, bottom-

81 Exactly not unlike Messrs. French and Belvedere.

82 Although those probably weren't the best two rhyming examples to use; they look pretty similar. Sorry.

talcuming, night-capping, and tucking-in need—I would probably hate even more than I already do.

But, as they say, good help is hard to find.

And so, when you find a good valet, you should go to great lengths to keep him. Because this quiet, often inexplicably-depressed old man is going to be responsible for getting you out of bed and then out the door of the penthouse—every morning —looking and feeling and smelling like the stuff dreams are made of. He will also, not that you give it any real thought whatsoever, become the closest thing to a friend that you have in the world. A realization which . . .

(Please excuse me a moment. I have something in my eye.)

Okay, I'm back. Now that we've defined what a valet *is*, let's discuss what a valet *does*.

In a word: *everything*.

In addition to preparing sumptuous repasts on which for you to feast (see *Recipes*, page 125, in the *How to Dine* section), your valet will ensure that your penthousehold runs smoothly: he will do the liquor shopping, the other shopping, the laundry, and the cleaning. He will run all the errands; provide your female guests with a lemon-scented moist towelettes and bag lunches as they tiptoe barefoot—having no idea where their shoes ended up, because shit got crazy in here last night—out the door in the morning; feed your lemur; and also pay all the bills (although he will probably pad these totals, to feed another monkey: the one on his frail, liver-spotted back).

He will—if you allow him to do so, which I do not—lay out your clothes every morning and every evening. He will remove bloodstains from anything: your sofa, your piqué shirt, your sheets, even the flawless Pennsylvania Bluestone with which your breathtaking terrace is paved.

He will make you a grilled-cheese sandwich. *At any hour of the day or night.*

He will personally shave you. And not only your face: whatever area of your body you feel may benefit from a moment's attention with a razor and a dollop of homemade shave cream. This may seem strange—or even frightening—at first, but don't worry: a taste of his spoon-cooked Burmese medicine and those arthritic old hands will be steady as a rock. And besides, this kind of blindly devoted, utterly personal attention is exactly what you're paying your valet for.

Although, now that I think about it, I'm not even sure that Woodhouse *gets* paid. I certainly don't write him a check every two weeks. In fact, also now that I think about it, I don't even *have* checks.[83]

So yeah, I don't know: I guess he just does it out of love.

FAMOUS VALETS AND BUTLERS, RANKED BY LEVEL OF AWESOMENESS

1. Jeeves
2. Kato
3. Alfred Pennyworth
4. Mr. Belvedere
5. Passepartout
6. Every other butler/valet in the history of mankind (tie)

∞. Woodhouse

---

83 Hey, where do you guys get your checks? Will the bank or whoever let you have king cobras printed on them?

ARCHER BY THE NUMBERS: WOODHOUSE

- Age of Woodhouse (in human years): 150 (estimated)
- Weight of Woodhouse (naked and crying, in pounds): 103
- Height of Woodhouse (in feet and inches): 5′3″
- Height of Woodhouse (in hobbits): 1.3
- Amount I would pay to see Woodhouse fight a hobbit: $100,000[*]

[*] I would earn all that back by betting on the hobbit.[†]

[†] Shit, but who'd bet on Woodhouse?[‡]

[‡] Oh. I'll just make him bet on himself. Duh.

CLOTHES

Hi. Look down. What do you see?

I am hoping—against all hope—that you see a necktie. If you do not, please put this book down and get back to work: that drainage ditch isn't going to dig itself. If you *do* see a necktie, but its color is lighter than—or, God forbid, *the same as*—the color of your shirt, please put this book down and get back to work: you're probably late to a Mafia staff meeting.

If you see a necktie which is *darker* than your shirt, please continue reading.[84]

Are you still reading?

Great. Hi again. Now please allow me to point out an uncomfortable truth: you should be spending more on clothes.

I don't care what you're wearing, if it's not what *I'm* wearing—and, mind you, I'm not talking about the actual *garments*: I'm talking about the *fibers* that were either hand-picked or hand-shorn from a variety of plants and/or animals, then hand-woven (or hand-knitted) into the *cloth* that was then purchased by a buyer, on behalf of your bespoke tailor; and then cut into the *fabric* which was then, after numerous fittings

84 Unless that tie is knotted in a half-Windsor. If this is the case, you are probably a child and thus should not be reading this book. Although if you *are* a child, and have made it this far (without skipping ahead!) you're probably going to eventually become an absolutely kickass man-adult, so keep reading: pretty soon we get into whores.

and refittings, sewn into an actual *garment*—then you might as well just be buying your bullshit off the rack.

From whatever men's outlet is closest to the drainage ditch you're currently digging.

But once you've saved up enough of your hard-earned ditch-digging wages, follow me to a select few bespoke tailors on—and actually just *off* of, for those in the know—Savile Row.

Which is in London. Which is in England. Which is a country that I normally consider laughably incompetent in every other single facet of every other single thing—from cuisine to cocktails to architecture to espionage to fighting world wars to having hot women—but is the only country in which you should ever have your suits and shirts *made for you*. By a bespoke tailor.

Because even though England pretty much sucks at everything else, by some miracle, it breeds the best tailors in the world. It also breeds the best butlers, valets, chauffeurs, footmen, charwomen, and many other incredibly servile professions. Spies, obviously, not so much.

And while I don't have the space—not to mention the inclination—to thoroughly explain every single facet of men's fashion to you, here are some basic guidelines to get you started.

BESPOKE TAILORS

Go to London and stop a rich guy on the street (he'll have a bowler hat and an umbrella) and ask him who his tailor is. Then make him take you there.

SUITS

Although I don't recommend it, you can probably squeak by with twelve. Three for each season, though obviously you can adjust that ratio depending on the climate where you live. English, American or French cut; pleats or flat fronts; cuffed hems or plain; lapel widths; double or single vent . . . I can't tell you what you need, because I don't know what your body looks like. That's why you're paying your bespoke tailor thousands and thousands of dollars to fuss around and take all those measurements and get chalk everywhere and sometimes touch your genitals: no matter how ridiculous your body type, this little hobbit of a man is going to make you look good.

FORMAL WEAR

The French call a tuxedo *un smoking*, which for some reason totally delights me. And as with your suits, it may seem like a lot, but the minimum number of tuxedos you need is this: two. Plus two white dinner jackets on top of that, which—somewhat confusingly—should never actually be white, but rather ivory or bone. I prefer a shawl collar on my formal jackets, but you may wish to choose a notched or peaked lapel on yours. The peaked lapel is generally considered the more formal option, but it really doesn't matter which style of lapel you choose: everyone, including your date and/or wife, will probably be looking at me.

The tuxedo is worn with a bow tie, which should be no more than one-and-a-half inches wide. This is so it looks cooler when it's untied later in the evening (or now, or whenever) when you're shitfaced. It's also worn with "braces" (not "suspenders," unless you're Uncle Jesse) and a cummerbund, the pleats of which should face upward. This is so you can stash some Goldfish crackers in there.

If your invitation says "black tie," that's what it means: your tie and cummerbund should be *black*. If your invitation says "white tie," that's this whole other thing, but I wouldn't even worry about it if I were you, because you're probably never going to get an invitation that says that.

SHIRTS

Your bespoke tailor will recommend a bespoke shirtmaker. Go there. With fabric swatches from your (minimum of twelve) new suits. Get measured. Laugh heartily when your shirtmaker asks, "Button cuffs or link, sir?" But then get serious when he asks, "Single or French?" because the question of single cuff versus French cuff is no laughing matter. After discussing each type's strengths and weaknesses with your shirtmaker, just order about thirty of each. And throw in about a dozen tuxedo shirts because these inevitably get stained by red wine and/or prostitute fluids.

ARCHER FUN FACT: THIS BOOK

I only have to write twelve thousand more words. Blah blah blah blah. There's four of them.

NECKTIES

Neckties should always be handwoven of Thai silk from the wild *Saturniidae* silkworm, and thus frightfully expensive. They should also be *neckties*. You should only wear a *bow tie* if the rest of the clothes on your body are a tuxedo. You should only wear a *string tie* if you invented fried chicken. There is no reason whatsoever to ever wear a *bolo tie*. None, not one.

The width of the lapels on your bespoke suits will determine the width of your neckties. The collars on your custom shirts and—to a somewhat lesser extent—the shape of your face will determine the knot you should use. I personally prefer the full Windsor or the Pratt, for example, but a double Windsor may look better on you. With that big fat pumpkin face of yours.

ACCESSORIES

Belts: The belt loops on your bespoke suits will determine the width of your custom belts, which should be handcrafted from some type of animal hide that you're embarrassed to even say out loud (a fawn, a newborn calf, a koala bear, etc.).

Cuff links: As with all choices concerning personal style, you should strive for understated elegance. Tiny snow globes are neither understated nor elegant. Tiny silver skulls are neither. Anything related to hunting and/or fishing is neither. And unless you're going to a black-tie function on an Indian reservation—which I bet they probably don't even have—avoid cuff links made of turquoise.

Pocket squares: This is the handkerchief that goes in the breast pocket of your suit, and there is a reason it's called a pocket "square" and not a pocket "frilly shitwad." That's because the only fold you should ever use is the square fold—also known as the Presidential—which should extend exactly three-eighths of an inch above, and perfectly parallel to, your breast pocket. Any other fold—the Two-Point, the Dunaway, the Flute, and don't even get me started on the Puff—is an abomination.

Note: In addition to your pocket square, always keep a separate clean cotton handkerchief folded in the pocket of your trousers. Because at some point in the evening, through no (or some, or total) fault of your own, your date is probably going to start crying.

Jewelry: Sure, pick some up on the way home from your gender-reassignment surgery.

ARCHER FUN FACT: NECKWEAR

Neckties were invented by the Croats during the Thirty Years' War in the sixteenth century. In fact, the word "cravat" comes from the Croatian word *Hrvati,* which I thought was a kind of cheese but is apparently what Croats call themselves. I guess because they're too busy losing wars to learn English.

SHOES

So, you're out buying shoes, huh? Neat! Seriously, that's great; I'm sure you're pretty excited. But before buying them, take just a brief moment to look around: Are you in Italy?

If not, *stop what you're fucking doing.*

Because the only place you should *ever* buy shoes, in the universe and beyond, is Italy. And that's not even accurate: you shouldn't even *buy* shoes. You should have them *made*. By a *cordwainer*. And, if possible, that cordwainer should possess the strong yet supple hands of the irascible yet avuncular Signore Antonio Carbone of Casa di Scarpe Carbone, in Firenze.[85]

Because Antonio—which I can, after fourteen years, only just now call him—will bring you into his well-appointed shop just off the Via Tornabuoni and talk with you—over an espresso followed by a grappa or two—about what it is, exactly, that you're looking for in a shoe: Day or evening? Lace-up or slip-on? Do you foresee driving while wearing the shoe? Dancing? Lovemaking?

He will listen intently. And perhaps even nod gravely. He will then beckon for you to follow him to the back of the shop, where you will—in addition to being utterly seduced by the buttery aroma of hand-softened cordovan—be measured for a pair of his sublime footwear.

---

85 Which you probably call *Florence*. Because I still want to murder you.

Each foot will be measured separately, at no fewer than twenty-six points—during which Antonio may even inquire into your dietary habits and/or family medical history. These measurements will be related to Antonio's positively *ancient* assistant, who will silently enter them into a well-worn ledger, bound in the softest calfskin and containing the foot measurements of kings, dukes, princes, viscounts, captains and/or titans of industry, and also the world's greatest secret agent.[86]

Antonio's assistant will prepare a *copia* of these measurements, which will then be taken into the basement by one of Antonio's young nephews, who will use them to create wooden lasts, one for each of your feet, using kiln-dried wood from the very heart of an old-growth Claret Ash.

As the nephew slips eagerly downstairs to hand-carve your lasts, you will be shown a dizzying array of exquisite leathers, from which you will be asked to choose your upper. When you are asked, you will do Antonio a great kindness—and yourself an even greater favor—if you defer to the judgment of *il maestro calzolaio:* he knows not only what you want, but also what you need. At this point, more espresso and grappa will be served. And perhaps some biscotti.

You will then be asked to choose the *patina* which will grace the impossibly supple leather of your uppers. Don't be afraid of making a mistake here: not only will Antonio gently nudge you toward the correct choice, he can also—should you ever decide to—change the patina (via a secret process known only to him) using a proprietary blend of plant- and oil-based dyes.

You will then—after a brief consultation, over more espresso and grappa—be asked to choose a type of sole. The sole you choose will (obviously) depend on when and where

---

86 Me.

you foresee wearing the shoes, but as ever, Antonio will be delighted to assist you in making the correct choice. The style and materials of your bespoke shoes having been carefully selected, the entire staff of Casa di Scarpe Carbone will join you in a toast over a glass of delicate prosecco.

Three to four weeks later, you will receive your shoes—in a handcrafted, velvet-lined box made from the wood of a young Atlas Cedar—along with a handwritten note from Antonio:

Signore Archer, mio caro amico: si prega di godere di questa umile offerta di scarpe. —A.

Note: Be prepared to spend a little more for shoes like this.

PERSONAL GROOMING

I am constantly astounded by the fact that some men—men who are sometimes, though not often, nearly as impeccably dressed as *I* am—overlook their personal grooming habits. Because a woman isn't going to notice that your Sulka tie has a perfect knot (a fact she should instantly recognize) if the nose above that knot looks like a gerbil ran up there and got stuck.

HAIR

Kept short. And also naturally thick and with a luxuriant sheen. Nothing else will do.

BATHING

Using handmade, lavender-scented Aleppo (note that I did not say Castile) soap, your valet will bathe you from head to toe, including your hair: the olive and laurel oils in Aleppo soap will lend to your hair's naturally (if you are me) luxuriant sheen. Don't worry about your being bathed by your valet seeming homoerotic: If anything, he will be oddly detached and clinical throughout the entire process. Almost as if he finds the very act to be incredibly distasteful.

FRAGRANCE

Bay rum with lime. Only. Ever. I shouldn't have to say that. Now I'm furious again.

NAILS

Fingernails and toenails should be kept clipped short, with no protrusion past the tip of their respective digits. Cuticles should be pushed back, frequently yet carefully, and preferably immediately following a hot shower or bath, which will make them more pliable. And if this sounds like a mani-pedi, that's because it is. And which your valet will perform for you on a weekly basis. And also which, in addition to being important to good overall nail health, is also a great opportunity to sit back, sip a smoky glass of single-malt scotch, and mock your valet. For having to kneel down, on his nearly glass-like kneecaps, and dig out a bunch of your toe jam.

SHAVING

I used to go to this great place down on Twenty-eighth and Seventh. Little hole-in-the-wall run by a Russian émigré and staffed by his two daughters: fantastic hot-towel, straight-razor shaves. But then the two daughters caught pregnant and had

to be shipped off to relatives in Michigan, and the few times I went back after that, he was bordering on impolite. Now Woodhouse shaves me.

Straight razor only. The blade is Solingen steel, hollow-ground, French-tipped, and stropped on only the finest leather. The handle is elk antler.[87] The brush is (and can only be) silver-tip badger: this is my face we're talking about. The shave cream is a proprietary blend of Woodhouse's own creation, the ingredients of which I promised I would not divulge herein.

A note about facial hair: *No.*

Unless you are a cop, Latino, or some combination thereof. In which case it is acceptable for you to have a mustache. A Van Dyke beard (often erroneously called a goatee) is acceptable only if you are an evil mastermind. Which, if you are reading this book, I hope you are not.[88]

---

87 Don't ask me what kind of elk, I have no idea. But I just assume it's a German one; the blade was made there, and historically the Germans have been pretty good at maximizing economies of scale. Just usually in really horrifying ways.

88 Because I feel like I've been pretty blabby. Secrets-wise.

PHYSICAL FITNESS

I don't know what to tell you about physical fitness. Because as unfair as it may be, I never, ever, ever work out, yet I look like Michelangelo carved me out of flesh-colored marble.

It's ridiculous. I can't even take my shirt off in developing countries (which are usually oppressively hot and humid, and thus the exact sort of place one most wishes to be shirtless) because I am instantly mobbed by tiny, snaggletoothed peasant women trying to wash their raggedy laundry on my glistening, rock-hard abs. Which is pleasurable for about two minutes, and then just becomes annoying. That being said, it is a great way to catch up on village gossip. And as anyone who knows me will tell you, I am an absolutely *incorrigible* gossip. It doesn't even have to be about a celebrity or even someone I know, I just love to hear it. Scandalous!

Obviously my profession is a fairly physically demanding one: scaling palace walls, fast-roping from helicopters, engaging in hand-to-hand combat with elite Spetsnaz paratroopers, the constant banging of exotic and mysterious women (many of whom are half my age)—these are all pretty strenuous activities. So I guess I get more exercise during the course of a normal business day than say, a stockbroker. Or a dentist. Or a teacher. Or . . . Well, you know what all the jobs are.

But even that doesn't explain the fact that if I were a Greek god back in ancient Rome, and Zeus caught Aphrodite feeding me pomegranate seeds, he'd be so jealous he'd turn me into a swan. I mean, all I do is eat rich restaurant food and drink enough alcohol, daily, to kill Ireland, and I *still* look like an underwear model. I guess I just have fantastic genes.

But as for you, I don't know. Maybe join a gym.

SECTION FOUR

HOW TO DINE

I was supposed to write an introduction to this section. But the title seems pretty self-explanatory. And also I didn't feel like it.

DINING OUT

I generally eat out. I know, I know, I've heard all the arguments against it: it's a waste of money, you have no control over how much salt and saturated fats are in restaurant food, and you can't be sure you're eating locally. But, if I may, let me respond to each of those arguments:

1. Expense account.
2. I'm pretty sure that any chef in any restaurant with at least two stars in the *Guide Michelin* knows how much salt and saturated fat is supposed to go into my exquisite meal.
3. Kill yourself.

I also consider myself an adventurous diner: for example, occasionally I like to seek out rickety shacks way out in the swampcountry where you get to eat barbecue and/or catfish with genial black people.[89] But normally I prefer to dine only in the finest restaurants of New York, Chicago, the Orient, France, and the nicer capitals of Europe. The only problem is that, with a lot of the very finest restaurants, especially if they have only very recently opened to smash reviews, it can be very difficult to get a reservation. And it may surprise you to

89 That sounded a lot less racist in my head.

learn that dropping the name Sterling Archer, the world's greatest secret agent, doesn't necessarily secure one a table.

Which is why I have perfected a method of reservation-making with which I am always assured of getting not just any table, but the very best table: the Abracadabra.

Start by calling (or having your valet call) that hip new restaurant everyone's raving about. Oh, the restaurant will probably have two reservation lines: one number for rich, glamorous, beautiful people in the know and a second number for people like you. Usually the second number isn't even connected to an actual phone, and it will just ring and ring on your end. So you need to get your (or your valet's) hands on the first number. For people who matter.

Call that number and tell the young woman on the other end—who you can just tell is not only ridiculously hot but also impeccably dressed—that you wish to make a reservation for Friday night at nine o'clock. After her eyes roll audibly, tell her you're calling from Capitol Records, and that you wish to make a reservation for Steve Miller.

"*The* Steve Miller?" she asks, sitting up a little straighter.

"And a stunning female companion," you reply.

"Friday at nine it is, sir. Does Mr. Miller have any food allergies the chef should be aware of?"

"No, but he's a bit over chefs who feel like they have to turn everything into a foam."

Then, Friday night at nine (or whenever: they're not going to release your table), show up at the restaurant with your stunning female companion and tell the equally stunning hostess[90] that there should be a reservation for two under your name. Which is Steve Miller.

---

[90] If she happens to be *more* stunning, it is perfectly acceptable to dump your date and ask the hostess to dine with you.

Then allow yourself to be led to the best table in the entire restaurant, where you will be served a fantastic meal, fawned over, and possibly asked to explain what a pompatus is.

I know what you're asking yourself: How could this possibly work? When they see you, they're going to know that you are not, in fact, Steve Miller. Well, also ask yourself this: do *you* know what Steve Miller looks like?

No, you don't. Nobody does. He could be standing right next to you on the subway platform, playing "Jungle Love" on a custom Stratocaster with his name inlaid on the fretboard in mother-of-pearl, and you still wouldn't know who he is. Because as far as you or anybody else knows, Steve Miller is a big blue space-horse with a mane made out of orange space-flames.

But *everybody* loves him.

And *nobody* is going to make an ass out of himself (or especially herself) questioning the bona fides of a man claiming to be the original Gangster of Love. Because chances are if they didn't lose their virginity to "Rock'n Me," they lost it to "Wild Mountain Honey."

Now, obviously the Abracadabra is geared toward white men.[91] It won't work if you're a woman. I can't think of a female multiplatinum recording artist you could use in lieu of the Space Cowboy, but it doesn't really matter: if you're a woman you're probably not reading this book. If you're a black guy, your best bet is probably Peabo Bryson.

---

91 I've also had some success posing as Boz Scaggs. Two people the Abracadabra will *not* work with, however, are Bob Seger (because people are pretty sure you're supposed to have a beard) and Jethro Tull (because he's dead).

STEVE MILLER BAND ALBUMS, RANKED BY LEVEL OF AWESOMENESS

1. *Greatest Hits 1974–1978*
2. The rest of them (tie)

DINING IN

Sometimes, albeit rarely, I don't feel like going to all the trouble of getting all dressed up and going out for dinner. When this happens, which is rarely, I get all dressed up and stay in for dinner. Breakfasts I'm usually home for, unless I'm on a mission. Same thing for brunch. Same thing for this new thing people are doing called dunch. But I never—*ever*—eat lunch at home.[92]

But the great thing about dining at home, if you're me, is that you live in well over four thousand square feet of a richly appointed penthouse overlooking Central Park (not including almost 900 square feet of terrace, paved with flawless Pennsylvania Bluestone), so you know the ambience is going to be nothing short of smashing. The other great thing is that—again, if you're me—you also have a valet who, having lived through the Siege of Ladysmith, knows how to whip up an incredible meal—often with remarkably few ingredients on hand, and also often at a moment's notice.

Because a moment's notice is normally all I give the creaking old fiend.

And so here—for the first time ever, and only because I can't really see a downside to sharing this information with you people—are Sterling Archer's favorite recipes.

92 Because I don't have a vagina.

RECIPES

Eggs Woodhouse

Happiness, thy name is Eggs Woodhouse! Each bite is a symphony of flavor: the fresh eggs and creamy sauces the percussion, the delightful Pata Negra ham the brass, both content to give the strings and woodwinds, the Périgord truffle and Beluga caviar, their respective solos. And the maestro who created this magnificent triumph, and who brings it to the stage each morning—accompanied by a pitcher of Bloody Marys, wheat toast with lemon curd, and a slice of melon—is none other than my loyal valet, Woodhouse.

By a cruel twist of fate, however, Woodhouse doesn't even know I've named the dish after him. I just say "Make me eggs."

- 1 cup creamed spinach (see recipe below)
- ½ cup béchamel (see recipe below)
- ½ cup hollandaise (see recipe below)
- 2 poached eggs (see recipe below)
- 2 artichoke bottoms (Blanc d'Oran or Camus de Bretagne)
- 2 ounces Pata Negra ham
- 1 small Périgord truffle

To Garnish

Pinch of paprika
(Édes csemege or Csípös Csemege, Pikáns)
1 teaspoon Beluga caviar
Pinch of Kashmiri saffron

Creamed Spinach

1 cup farm-fresh organic spinach
½ teaspoon freshly ground black pepper
¼ teaspoon sea salt (preferably sel de mer haïtien)

Cook the spinach, drain well, chop finely. Season with pepper and salt. Keep warm, while stirring constantly over a low flame until you add it to the béchamel (see recipe below).

Béchamel

1 tablespoon butter
(beurre d'Ardenne or Mantequilla de Soria)
1 tablespoon organic wheat flour
⅓ cup organic whole milk
1 bay leaf
4 dashes hot sauce
½ teaspoon sea salt (preferably sel de mer haïtien)

In heavy saucepan over low heat, melt—but do not brown—the butter. *Gradually* add flour, stirring constantly with a wire whisk. When all the flour is blended in, gradually pour in the milk, again stirring constantly. Add the bay leaf and simmer over low heat, stirring constantly, until the sauce thickens. Remove from heat, add hot sauce and salt, and continue stirring constantly.

Combine the spinach and béchamel sauce and keep warm, over a low flame, stirring constantly.

Hollandaise

1 organic, grain-fed, free-range white-egg yolk
¾ tablespoons freshly squeezed lemon juice
¼ cup clarified butter
(beurre d'Ardenne or mantequilla de Soria)
Sea salt (preferably sel de mer haïtien), to taste

In a separate copper-bottomed sauté pan, bring 3 cups distilled water to a simmer. Combine the egg yolk and 1 tablespoon *cold* distilled water in a nonreactive bowl. Whisk until delicately foamy, then whisk in a few drops of the freshly squeezed lemon juice. Set the bowl *over*—not *on*—the simmering water, until the egg begins to emulsify. Remove from heat and add clarified butter, just a few drops at a time, while gently whisking *constantly*. As the sauce thickens, begin to add the butter (only very slightly) more quickly until the rest is added. Gently whisk in remaining lemon juice, seasoning to taste.

Poached Eggs

1 tablespoon distilled white vinegar
2 organic, grain-fed, free-range *brown* eggs

In a separate copper-bottomed sauté pan, bring 2 inches distilled water and 1 tablespoon vinegar to a shimmer. Gently break each egg into an individual ramekin. Gently slide each egg from its individual ramekin into the shimmering water-vinegar bath and cook, occasionally spooning some of the bath over each egg, for 2 to 2½ minutes. Remove the eggs from the bath with a fine-mesh spoon.

Assembling the Dish

In a separate copper-bottomed sauté pan, warm the artichoke bottoms and set aside. In a separate copper-bottomed sauté pan, warm slices of the Pata Negra ham and set aside. In a separate copper-bottomed sauté pan, gently warm the Périgord truffle and set aside. Chiffonade the Pata Negra ham. Slice the truffle—exceedingly thinly, and only ever on the bias—using a double-edged razor blade (Gillette or Wilkinson).

Place the warm creamed spinach on a warmed plate, forming a sort of bed on which the other ingredients will make love. Place the warmed artichoke bottoms on the spinach bed and place a poached egg on each artichoke bottom. Over the eggs and artichokes, sprinkle the Pata Negra ham chiffonade and the thinly sliced Périgord truffle. Ladle the warm Hollandaise sauce over the dish. Garnish with the paprika, Beluga caviar, and Kashmiri saffron. (Serves 1.)

Note: I don't know—and I'm not sure I *want* to know!—the nutritional information for Eggs Woodhouse, but if properly prepared using the specified ingredients, each serving should cost around $130.

That's the only recipe: like I said, I normally eat out.[93]

93 Plus this isn't a cookbook.

SECTION FIVE

Like unarmed combat, personal style and airboat captaincy, the subject of women is probably another area where I am starting at an entirely different level from normal human men. Which makes it difficult—if not impossible—for me to give a normal human man, like yourself, any practical advice on the matter. That would be akin to a majestic white Bengal Tiger trying to teach you how to be more majestic. Or how to be heterozygous for a specific recessive gene.

I know you probably bought this book for advice on how to be like me.[94] But to be perfectly honest—which I sincerely believe I have tried to somewhat be—I cannot teach the unteachable. I can (although I didn't) teach you how to tie a perfectly knotted Pratt or Windsor. I can (although I didn't) teach you how to increase the effective kill radius of a Claymore anti-personnel mine by almost 10 percent (there's a little set-screw). And I can (although I won't) teach you how to drive an airboat, and look like a million bucks plus Burt Reynolds while doing so.

What I emphatically *cannot* do is teach you how to be successful with women. For one thing, as devastatingly handsome as I personally am, I really don't want a bunch of competition. For another thing: look at yourself.

That being said, however (and I do feel that I've been very honest with you), I will try.

[94] In your defense, I can see how the book's title is maybe a little misleading

AMATEURS

By "amateurs," I don't mean women who are less-than-adept in the ways of love: I just mean non-hookers. And many, many, many, many women who don't get *paid* to have sex are nonetheless pretty great at it. And these women are simply everywhere: in bars, at the market, at your job, in a doctor's waiting room, on the bus[95], the wife of your host at a lavish dinner party . . . Name the location, and chances are there's a hot woman there willing to have sex with ~~me~~ you.

I know, you're thinking: "Are you serious? At my *job*? That seems like a terrible idea."

---

95 You strike me as the sort of person who would be caught dead on a bus.

Really? The place where you spend forty hours a week? Almost a third of the waking hours of your adult life? And you want to make that a sex-free zone? Are *you* serious?

Because there is absolutely no valid reason why you shouldn't be systematically banging your way through the entire steno pool. If your employer has rules against this sort of thing, just lie about it. If you're worried that a workplace sexual relationship will inevitably sour—which it will—just get her fired. This is easy to do, if you had the foresight to start stringing along your chubby, cardigan-wearing director of human resources, who will leap at the chance to eliminate her perceived competition. If you lacked this foresight, just put some drugs in her locker.[96]

Wherever you're trying to bang these women (which should be everywhere), the key, as with pretty much every single other thing that you ever do in your entire life, is confidence. My confidence comes from the fact that I am not only devastatingly handsome but also the world's greatest secret agent. I can't help you with either of those two things, but I can give you some field-tested pickup lines (although I hate that phrase), in several of the world's sexier languages:

Afrikaans	*Ek is 'n geheime agent. Wil jy 'n seks te hê met my?*
Czech	*Jsem tajný agent. Chtěli byste mít sex se mnou?*
Dutch	*Ik ben een geheim agent. Wil je seks met mij?*
Euskadi	*Agente sekretu bat naiz. Nahi al duzu sexuaren dute nirekin?*

[96] You also strike me as the sort of person who works in a place where they have lockers.

French	*Je suis un agent secret. Voulez-vous coucher avec moi?*
German	*Ich bin ein Geheimagent. Möchten Sie die Sex mit mir haben?*
Italian	*Io sono un agente segreto. Ti piacerebbe fare sesso con me?*
Lithuanian	*Aš esu slaptas agentas. Ar norėtumėte turėti seksą su manimi?*
Portuguese	*Eu sou um agente secreto. Gostaria de fazer sexo comigo?*
Romanian	*Sunt un agent secret. Doriţi să faci sex cu mine?*
Russian	*Я секретный агент. Хотите заняться сексом со мной?*
Spanish	*Soy un agente secreto. ¿Quieres hacer sexo conmigo?*
Suomi	*Olen salainen agentti. Haluaisitko seksiä kanssani?*
Swahili	*Mimi ni wakala wa siri. Je, wewe kama kufanya mapenzi na mimi?*
Swedish	*Jag är en hemlig agent. Vill du ha sex med mig?*
Welsh	*Yr wyf yn asiant cudd. A hoffech chi gael rhyw gyda mi?*

And don't bother plugging these into a translator on the internets (which is what I did), because they all mean the exact thing: *I am a secret agent. Would you like to have sex with me?*[97]

[97] Note: I did not include this phrase in Arabic. This was not because I do not find Arabic women sexy. In fact, quite the opposite. I did not include it because, A) this stupid word-processing software turned the Arabic phrase into wingdingery gibberish, and B) even if you're as sexy as I am, no matter how much an Arabic woman wants to have sex with you, she doesn't want it enough to get her buried up to her neck in sand and pummeled in the face with rocks all afternoon.

FOR THE LADIES

I realize that it's highly improbable that any women—including, hopefully, my mother—are reading this book. But in the unlikely event that you are a woman, and in the (infinitely more likely) event that you're a woman who's reading this book because you hope to one day—God willing—have sex with me, I thought it might be useful to include some tips about how to make your evening of pleasure as a sexual guest in my home not only magical, but also even more magical than that.

1. Please refrain from smoking (including on the terrace).
2. While it would be wise for you to carb up in advance, please bear in mind that I'm going to be pouring gallons of alcohol down you, so don't eat anything you won't mind vomiting up later.

3. Please do not engage my valet in conversation beyond curt responses to his inquiries as to whether or not you would like more alcohol. (Note: Said curt response should only be *yes*.)
4. There is a lemur somewhere in the penthouse: if you see him, please do *not* give him sugar.
5. Please do not use my bath towels: if I wanted to rub my face on your ass, I would have done it while you were asleep. Which, now that I think about it, would be impossible, because:
6. You are not to sleep here.
7. If *I* am sleeping, please do not be afraid to leave quietly. In fact, I greatly prefer this. As you are leaving, my valet will provide you with a lemon-scented moist towelette and a bag lunch.
8. If you feel the need to pass wind—which, after an intense session of my style of lovemaking, you probably will—please do so through a dryer sheet; you will find some in the nightstand.
9. Don't fall in love with me.

PROFESSIONALS

"I don't pay them for sex. I pay them to leave."
—George Bernard Shaw

Prostitution, like torture, can be an incredibly sensitive, often divisive subject. Unlike torture, however, it's awesome. Think about it: In exchange for money, which you probably embezzled from your agency or extorted from a double agent in the first place, you can have amazing, adventurous, anonymous sex with a beautiful woman—or two or more women. Or a man. Or a combination of women and men. No one is judging you here. This is a safe place.

You're probably asking yourself: "Wait, what am I missing? Can it be that simple?"

Yes. Don't overthink it. Just put your money on the dresser and get banging.

I'm kidding, of course: having sex with a prostitute is actually a bit more complicated than that. For one thing, don't *ever* put your money on the dresser: she will probably rob you.

Instead—if you don't have a standing account with an escort service, and are thus forced to use cash—before your prostitute arrives, hide your wallet under the mattress. And not just near the edge: push it as far toward the center as possible. Because at some point during the evening (probably while you're in the bathroom having your pre-coital bowel movement), she's going to look for it. Which is why the wallet is just a decoy: *Always keep your money in your sock.* And your socks on your feet. If she asks why you're keeping your socks on, just tell her you're chilly. Or to shut up, you're not paying her to talk.

What you *are* paying her for is limited only by your imagination. Or, more accurately, by whatever specific sexual acts that she is willing to perform, each of which will have a specific and non-negotiable price.[98] And although these prices may be high, under no circumstances should you attempt to haggle over them: not only is this insulting to her and the world's oldest profession, it makes you look like an enormous douchebag. It's also not very romantic.

And so, to re-cap: *you* decide what you want, *she* decides what you're going to get.[99]

What that ends up being is between you two consenting adults, in the privacy of your own home, Midtown hotel room, or possibly under a bridge. I can't choose your sexual predilections for you: I can barely keep track of my own. But this is another reason why prostitution is so phenomenal: it affords one the opportunity to experiment sexually without having things be all weird the next morning, when she can't even bring herself to look at you over the Eggs Woodhouse you're just trying to enjoy without all this brunch-ruining drama.

98 If she takes her work seriously, she'll have a rate-card.
99 Not unlike a real relationship. Am I right, fellas?

French, Greek, GFE, ATM, domination, ass worship, watersports, queening, shrimping, figging, snowballing, role-playing, crib-wetting, double penetration, shocking penetration, reverse cowgirl, reverse cowgirl-on-girl, girl-on-Woodhouse . . . The list is literally endless, and my point is: Don't be afraid to try new things. You might just surprise yourself. Although not her.

And while I could go on for literally thousands of pages, space prohibits me from delving into the customs and mores of international prostitution, which obviously differ from country to country. In Thailand for example, it is considered incredibly rude to touch a prostitute on the head. The good news is that, this being Thailand, they don't need any help from you.

So go get 'em, tiger. And always, always remember: *money in sock, socks on feet.*

ARCHER FUN FACT: THAI PROSTITUTES

The chances of your Thai prostitute being transgendered are about one in three. And while that statistic is entirely made up, the point I'm trying to make is who are you to judge?

THE ARCHER SUTRA

So, I had this whole big fantastic idea for this section: me and two glamorous cover models would be photographed on my terrace by a famous photographer—over the course of weeks, shooting only at what Terrence Malick and Stanley Kubrick have called the *golden hour*—as we engaged in dozens of various and exotic and amazing sexual positions.

Then—via computers—our glistening, ejaculate-splattered bodies would be turned into tasteful silhouettes, accompanied by the erotic-yet-instructional instructions that I was going to write. Probably would have saved marriages all over the world.

HarperCollins, not surprisingly, balked at the idea:

"We're not going to pay thousands of dollars to photograph you having sex with women," said my editrix, jealously.

"You mean *other* women," I said, admittedly cruelly.

"You're an asshole."

Well yeah, *now*. Because since HarperCollins wouldn't pony up, and actual cover models A) are incredibly expensive, and B) only work for modeling agencies where they slam the phone down in your ear when you tell them their models can expect to be splattered with ejaculate, I was forced to make my own silhouettes. And even though I worked really hard on them, the end result wasn't quite as erotic-yet-instructional as it would have been if HarperCollins had agreed to my original concept. Which, as we have learned, was to include semen-drenched cover girls.

But whatever: here's the Archer Sutra.

POSITION ONE: THE FLOWERING LOTUS

Yeah thanks, HarperCollins.

I literally spent three hours dicking around with the stupid drawing tool on this word-processing software just to make this one silhouette. But instead of a tasteful rendering of a handsome man introducing a beautiful woman to the subtle mélange of complex emotions and intense physical pleasure which is anal sex, I get a gingerbread centaur shitting out a soccer ball.

I'm bailing.

INTERNATIONAL SECRET
ISIS
INTELLIGENCE SERVICE
INTERNATIONAL SECRET
ISIS
INTELLIGENCE SERVICE
ISIS
INTELLIGENCE SERVICE

SECTION SIX

HOW TO PAY FOR IT

I'm not going to, but I bet if I read back over this book, I would realize that a lot of the advice in it is incredibly expensive. I mean, the Triple-A Power Play alone requires a hundred thousand dollars in working capital. And although you walk away with all of it—minus cab fare and however much it costs you to take an obnoxiously drunk herd of beet-faced Asians out for short ribs—you need to possess (or at least have temporary access to) that kind of money to begin with. Which I do.

But which a lot of you probably do not. Which is not my fault: I don't vote Democrat.[100]

[100] I actually don't vote at all. To learn more about this interesting fact, please turn the page.

PERSONAL FINANCE

Okay, I'm out of my skull with boredom (though I'm sure you're not) and the word count is looking pretty good, so I'm just going to breeze through this part. For a change.

The first thing you should do is assess your financial situation. Which I bet is shitty.

The next thing you should do is figure out a way to improve it. I would suggest, unless you are already a multi-millionaire, that you quit your job: it's obviously not getting you where you need to be, which is multi-millionairedom. Then go find a better job. Something that you like, but that also pays you assloads of money to show up at. And you're on your own with the job search: I'm not a guidance counselor. What I am is the world's greatest secret agent.

Which means that, in addition to my base salary (which is decent) and my bonuses (also decent), I have access to hundreds upon hundreds of thousands upon thousands of dollars (much more than decent). Because international espionage is an expensive proposition: night-vision goggles, 81mm rocket launchers, chartered flights, boutique hotels, high-end whores, ski passes, bullets, liquor, 81mm shells *for* the rocket launchers, helicopter gas . . . All this stuff costs money.

Which I am able to *expense*.

And I'm just going to assume that my mother is too green with jealousy to ever read this book, so I'll just go ahead and tell you that not only do I expense everything, I do so with about a 15 percent pad. In my experience, 15 percent is about as far as I can push it. Any more than that and my mother starts asking a lot of uncomfortable questions, like "Was it really necessary to charter a helicopter full of liquor and whores and 81mm rocket launchers to a ski resort?"[101]

But padding my operational expenses is only a drop in the bucket of—well, *embezzling* has kind of a negative connotation, so let's call it something else. Like *personal wealth-building*. And the bulk of my personal wealth has been built from diverting funds that were supposed to have gone toward bribing foreign operatives and officials. I know, it's hard to hear that: as with torture, you wince to think of your government's relying on bribery to further its political goals. Well, grow up: protecting your freedom, not unlike grinding doe-eyed calves into those fucking sliders you can't seem to get enough of, isn't pretty.

What *is* pretty is the fact that almost any foreign-intelligence operative (who, remember, are just mustachioed versions of me) or corrupt official will settle for less than the agreed-upon bribe: If he said he'd give you the schematics of his country's secret nuclear weapons facility for *three* million dollars, it's a safe bet that he'll give them to you for two. Especially with the barrel of a (beautifully made) Walther PPK in his mouth. The extra million goes into an untraceable bank account in the Caymans. Or the Isle of Man. I personally like to spread it around a little.

I know: you're wondering why I agreed to write this

---

101 No. (Duh.)

(impossibly long) book if I have millions of dollars salted away in secret numbered accounts all over the globe. Yeah, hi: Did you read this book? Or did you just skip ahead to this page? I don't have millions of dollars, dodo.

In fact, I hate to admit it but I pretty much live paycheck to paycheck. Mainly because I do things like rent $12,000 whores, eat a hundred bucks' worth of eggs every single morning of my damn life, and pay my tailor to widen the lapels—on every single suit that I own—one-sixteenth of an inch every autumn. Which I then pay to have *re-narrowed* one-sixteenth of an inch every spring.[102]

But, even though I'm a bit of a spendthrift, one area where you *won't* catch me wasting money is on taxes. I'm not (due to my lack of a vagina) a qualified tax advisor, so any advice which follows is merely for informational purposes. But if you pay taxes, you're an idiot.

And not only do I not *pay* taxes, I've never even filed a return. And I can't start now, because then they'll know I've never filed before. And in researching this kickass book, I learned that while failure to *pay* one's taxes is merely a misdemeanor (I think), failure to *file* a tax return is a *felony*. Which would mean I wouldn't be allowed to vote. Which I don't do.

Because the United States government doesn't even know I exist.

Well, they probably know I exist (especially now that I'm a bestselling author) but they don't know where to find me.

---

102 This is because I normally gain four to five ounces of unsightly winter fat every year, which all seems to go straight to my face, and I feel the wider lapel helps to balance the overall look. Although now that I think about it, I have dozens of fall/winter suits which are entirely separate and different from my dozens of spring/summer suits, so to pay to have them *all* altered is actually pretty stupid. See? We can all do a little better when it comes to saving.

And even if they did, good luck with *that*. But it's a moot point, because Sterling Malory Archer has never received taxable income of any sort whatsoever. Because when I was born, my mother was foresightful enough to bribe the relevant authorities into declaring that she gave birth to identical twin sons, one of whom lived only a few hours. Which was just long enough for him to receive both a notarized birth certificate and a Social Security number, before being given a tasteful burial (in a heartbreakingly small white coffin).

And so 100 percent of my taxable income, as well as any and all stocks, bonds, and property that I may own—including my 4,300 square-foot penthouse apartment overlooking Central Park—is actually in the name of my fictional deceased twin sibling: *Elvis Roosevelt Archer.*[103]

ARCHER FUN FACT: RACCOONS

Raccoons are just fun in general. To me, at least. Go write your own fucking book.

[103] Little Baby El-Ro, we called him.

APPENDIX A: MAPS

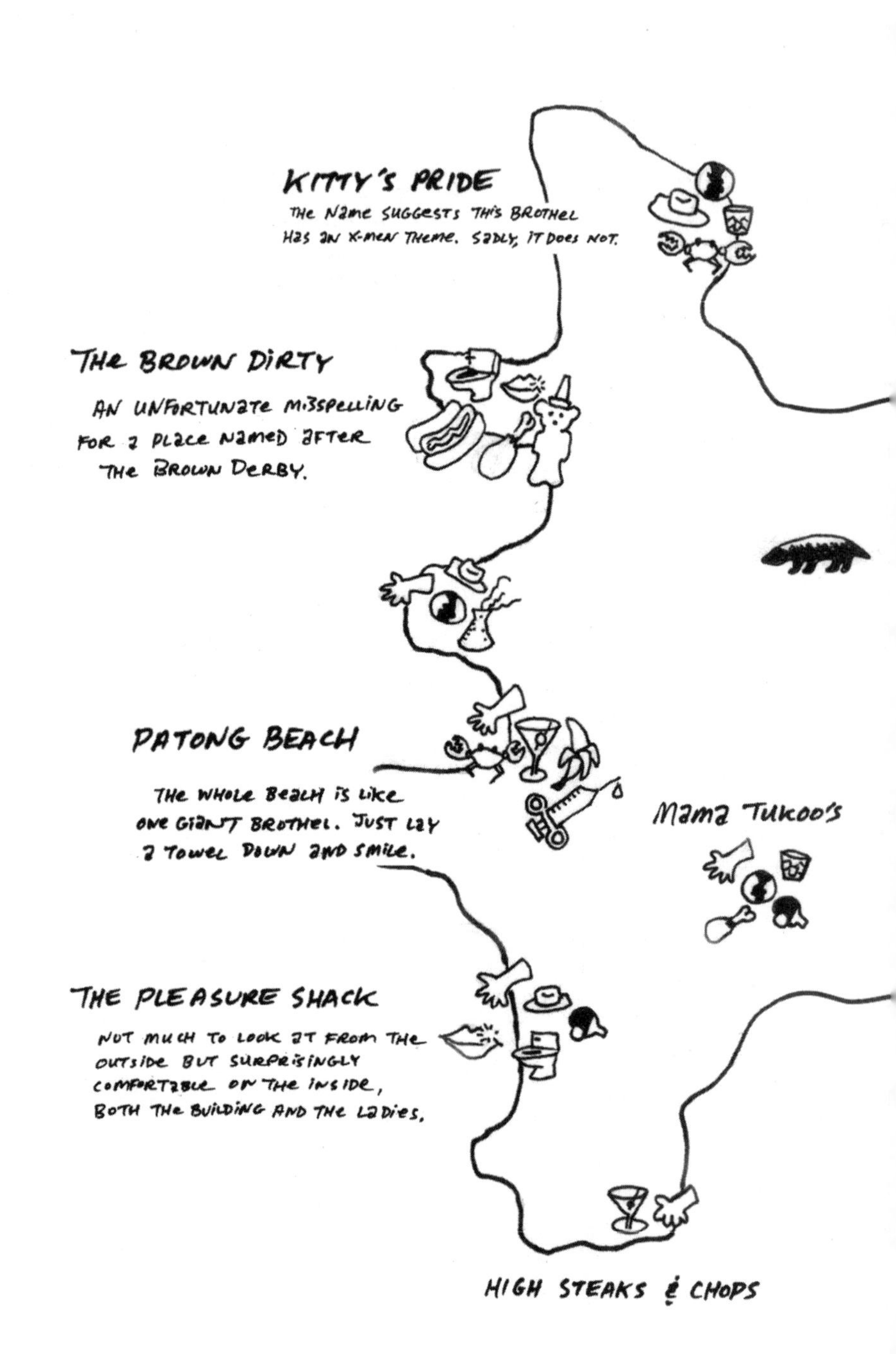
KITTY'S PRIDE
THE NAME SUGGESTS THIS BROTHEL HAS AN X-MEN THEME. SADLY, IT DOES NOT.
THE BROWN DIRTY
AN UNFORTUNATE MISSPELLING FOR A PLACE NAMED AFTER THE BROWN DERBY.
PATONG BEACH
THE WHOLE BEACH IS LIKE ONE GIANT BROTHEL. JUST LAY A TOWEL DOWN AND SMILE.
MAMA TUKOO'S
THE PLEASURE SHACK
NOT MUCH TO LOOK AT FROM THE OUTSIDE BUT SURPRISINGLY COMFORTABLE ON THE INSIDE, BOTH THE BUILDING AND THE LADIES.
HIGH STEAKS & CHOPS

WHOREHOUSES OF PHUKET, THAILAND

(COMPLETELY FROM MEMORY)

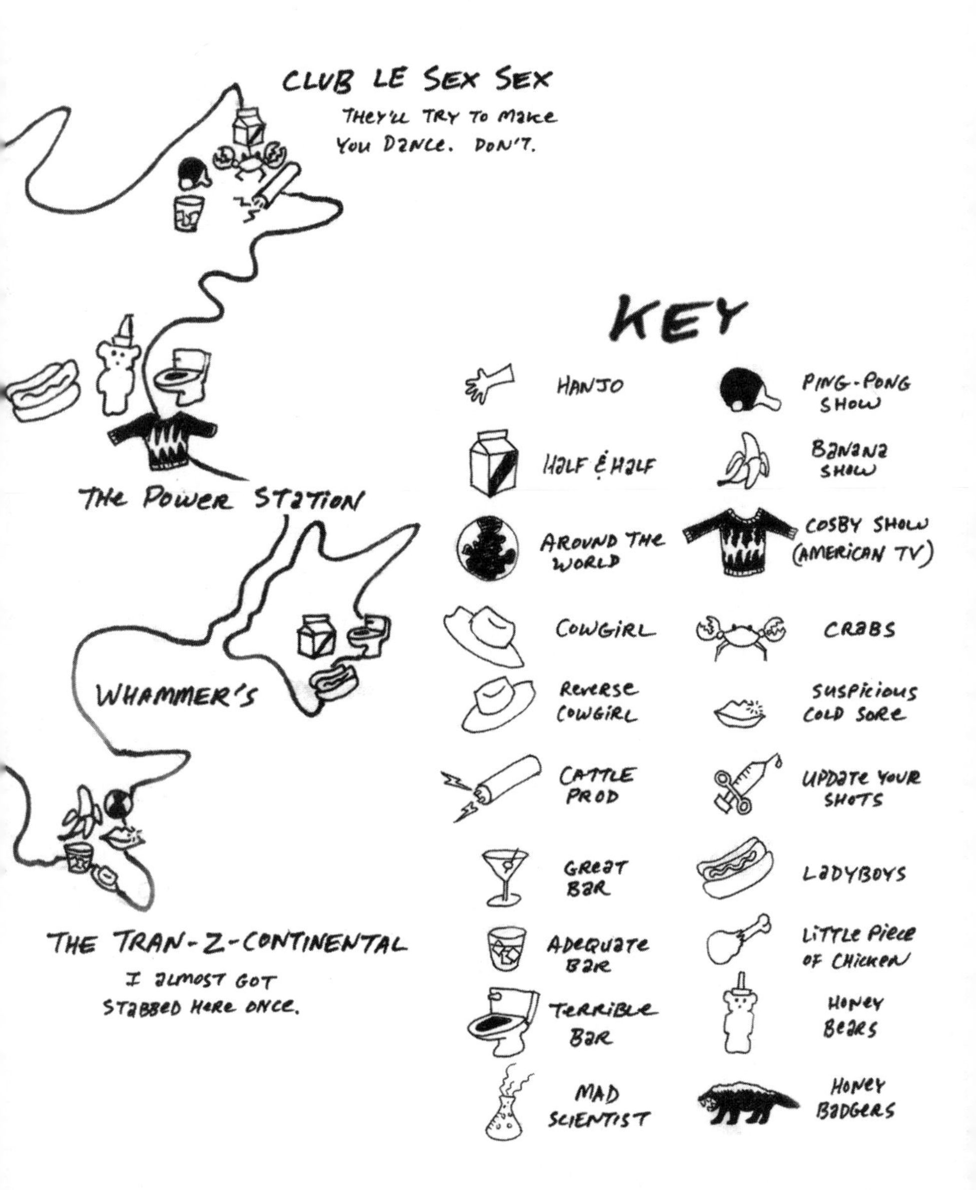

APPENDIX B: FIRST AID

Just go to a hospital.

APPENDIX C: ARCHER'S WORLD FACTBOOK

A brief compendium of useful information about several countries to which one could reasonably expect to travel in one's role as the world's greatest secret agent. And also, Canada.

ALBANIA

What's not to like about a nation that's not only covered with reinforced-concrete machine gun bunkers, but also formerly ruled by a king named Zog? Answer: everything else.

ANDORRA

This tiny principality is actually a *co*-principality, meaning it's ruled by two princes. Which makes me wonder: What ever happened to the Spin Doctors? Were they all murdered?

BOSNIA AND HERZEGOVINA

The country so nice they named it twice. Actually they just named it once, and that name is terrible. Which is fitting, because both Bosnia *and* Herzegovina are pretty terrible themselves.

CANADA

I like Quebec because it's just like being in France, only everybody drives pickup trucks. Plus, I heard all the Quebecoises are descended from actual French whores from a long time ago!

CÔTE D'IVOIRE

I don't care what it wants to be called, I'm still calling it the Ivory Coast. *Côte d'Ivoire* sounds like some type of cheese. The *Ivory Coast* sounds like something out of Middle Earth.

THE DOMINICAN REPUBLIC

No matter how poor a person in the Dominican Republic may be, they will normally laugh at their situation and say something like "Well I may live in a dirt-floored typhus incubator of a shack, but at least I'm not Haitian!" When this happens, it is appropriate to laugh along with them. (Actually you must laugh, or you will be suspected of being a Haitian sympathizer.)

ETHIOPIA

It is acceptable—even encouraged—to eat the tablecloth: don't worry; it's almost a food.

FRANCE

Please do not construe this as a lame attempt at humor: the fries are actually great. Thin-cut and fried in impossibly hot oil and sprinkled with sea salt, they're just amazing with *moules*.

THE GAMBIA

Not Gambia, *the* Gambia. And just like alumni of *the* Ohio State University, Gambians make a gigantic deal about pointing this out. And strangely, the mascot of both is the buckeye.

HUNGARY

Its capital, Budapest, is actually two separate cities: Buda and Pest. Its main exports are mainly agricultural: wheat, corn, paprika, sugar beets, canola oil, and Gabor sisters.

ICELAND

The national dish of Iceland is *hákarl*, which is a dead shark chunked into a hole on the beach, urinated on by people, covered with sand, and left to ferment for five months. Hard to believe their economy collapsed. What with all that rancid piss-shark readily available for export.

JAPAN

When entering a Japanese home, custom dictates that you remove your shoes. When riding on a Japanese train, custom dictates that you chain-smoke right near me the whole time.

KAZAKHSTAN

Sounds made-up.

LATVIA

During WWII, Latvia was invaded by the Soviet Union. And then by Nazi Germany. Then by the Soviets again. After a brief *reinvasion* by the Nazis, they finally chose the Soviets. In my opinion—although I'm no expert, by any means—this is why the women all have bangs.

MONGOLIA

By far, the best Mongolian beef I have ever tasted in my life was positively, absolutely, definitely, 100 percent *not* served to me in Mongolia. In fact, I'd avoid eating there altogether.

NICARAGUA

Another nation—along with the Dominican Republic and Cuba—whose national pastime, due to lengthy occupation by American soldiers, is baseball. And also whose women are mocha-skinned goddesses with whom I want nothing more in life than to have sex until my dick bleeds.

OMAN

I always get this confused with Oran. By which I mean Oran "Juice" Jones, whose hit single "The Rain" peaked at number nine on the Billboard Top 100 chart. Which should've been way higher.

PANAMA

Home to the world's most strategically important shipping canal, Panama is also great for blasting out of your car stereo as you drive down to Myrtle Beach, just *pounding* some beers.

PARAGUAY

Paraguay is often confused with Uruguay.

PERU

Peru is the native habitat of the endangered Spectacled Bear, the species that served as the inspiration for . . . Paddington Bear! Paddington Bear! Paddington Bear! Yay, Paddington!

QATAR

To be honest, Qatar only made the list because I'm pretty sure it's the only country in the world that starts with Q. It's basically the "xylophone" of world factbooks. And also very sandy.

ROMANIA

Once, while out for a jog through the diesel-choked streets of Bucharest, I was pulled down by a snarling pack of stray dogs. There's no joke here: this actually happened to me.

SOMALIA

In recent years, Somalia has gained a well-deserved international reputation for being home to a large number of pirates. Which is probably why Somalia is so stoked.

SWEDEN

You are going to be the ugliest person in the entire country. This is perfectly normal.

SOUTH AFRICA

South Africa has a bad reputation for its decades-long, often-brutal segregationist policy of apartheid. A policy which I never understood, because black chicks are just incredibly hot.

THAILAND[104]

Don't touch the whores on the head.

---

[104] Thailand used to be called Siam. Conjoined twins used to be called Siamese twins, because the first (well-known) conjoined twins, Chang and Eng, were from Siam. They made a pile of money working in freak shows, moved to America and bought a huge farm in North Carolina, married two sisters with whom they had a total of twenty-one children (ten for Chang and eleven for Eng), and owned a bunch of slaves. All of which I find pretty darn fascinating.

URUGUAY

Uruguay is often confused with Paraguay.

VATICAN CITY

Before you visit Vatican City, spend a little time in Nicaragua. Or Guatemala. Or El Salvador. Or Honduras. And then just walk around the Vatican, growing more and more furious.

THE WESTERN SAHARA

It may sound like a chain of casual-dining steak restaurants, but it's actually a war-torn desert region whose borders are hotly disputed by Morocco, Spain, and Mauritania. And so, like a casual-dining steak restaurant, there is absolutely no reason to ever go there ever.

XYLOPHONIA

Not a real country. If it were, I bet its national anthem would be "Dem Bones." Played by a grinning skeleton on his own ribs. Which is why we should launch a preemptive strike *now.*

YEMEN

Also pretty sandy. From what I hear.

ZAIRE

I used to go here when it was still called the Belgian Congo. Before the hipsters found out about it and ruined it. Like they do everything else.

AFTERWORD[105]

And so, finally, we come to the end of the book. Did you learn anything? I hope you did. Because man, I sure did. I learned that about 95 percent of the information in the book you just bought was readily available, for totally free, on the internets. The other 5 percent I just made up.

---

105 Who writes this? Wait, what? You're shitting me.

ACKNOWLEDGMENTS

I would like to thank my editrix at HarperCollins, whose name I never learned, for the countless hours she spent helping me shape my raw, visceral experiences as the world's greatest secret agent into a practical guide for all those young men and women who wish to follow in my footsteps and enter into the fascinating and often dangerous world of the clandestine services; my colleagues at ISIS, not only for their courage, honor, and sense of duty but also for their kind words of support as I delved into often painful memories to bring this book to life; my tireless manservant Woodhouse, whose blind willingness to cater to my every whim—no matter how whimsical, and often at great expense to himself, both financially and physically—made writing this book, if not possible, then at least a lot easier; and lastly, and yet most of all, I would like to thank my mother, the "unsinkable" Malory Archer, who gave me not only my life but also my calling: as the dashing prince consort to the seductive and deadly queen known as espionage.

I'd like to thank all those people. And I totally would if they'd actually done anything to help me write this goddamn book. But apart from a few snide comments—oh, and by the way, Mother, thanks ever so much for that touching foreword—nobody ever even mentioned it. And so now they're not getting mentioned, except to tell them all thanks for exactly fucking nothing.

All but you, internets.

SELECTED BIBLIOGRAPHY

I don't know what this is.

ABOUT THE AUTHOR

Sterling Archer is the world's greatest secret agent and now also probably a bestselling author. A world-class cocksman and former all-conference preparatory school lacrosse player, he divides his time among New York City, Monte Carlo, the Orient, several of the classier islands of the Caribbean, and Gstaad. This is his first book.[106]

---

106 And his last. This whole thing was a huge pain in the ass.[107]

107 Shit. That's only 29,797 words. Okay, so now we're doing this: cobra

---

cobra cobra. There. Now fuck off, HarperCollins.